PEEKABOO
Copyright © Lucy Myatt 2016

Book Design
Copyright © Uncle Frank Productions

Published in December 2016 by Uncle Frank Productions by arrangement with the author. All rights reserved with the author. The right of Lucy Myatt to be identified as Author of this Work has been asserted by her in accordance with the Copyright, Design sand Patents Act 1988.

First Edition

ISBN
978-1-326-88040-8

This book is a work of fiction. Names, characters, places and incidents either are products of the authors twisted imagination or are used fictitiously. Any resemblance to actual events or locales or persons living or dead, is entirely coincidental.
Except you Dave, you shit.

Design & Layout by Uncle Frank Productions
logo by Emily Salinas
Additional art by Marina Ortega Lorente

Uncle Frank Productions
3 Brick St
Liverpool, L1 0BP

www.unclefrankproductions.com

Dedicated to Ilan Sheady who inspired me and pushed me to finish my first book.

Also to my dad, who is responsible for my irrational fear of clowns.

"The clown furor will pass, as these things do, but it will come back, because under the right circumstances, clowns really can be terrifying"

-Stephen King

Story behind the story

Ilan got in touch with me one day stressed out and annoyed at some company requesting a poster for an upcoming project they were working on. They needed a clown drawn up for an movie poster.

They did not think to give him any guidelines on what the clown looked like other than half his face must be burnt. Ilan came up with this terrifyingly grotesque creature to find out, that when they originally approached him, they already had a model for the clown, which looked nothing like the monster Ilan had designed.

After hours of working on a new image that was also rejected as they chose to go for the artist who only charges in exposure. Emotionally battered and bruised he confided in me that he made the image look like a book cover so it could simply go into his portfolio and make him feel a little better about the whole ordeal.

An idea popped into my head that I could make a little story for him. We could print two copies out and it would be the ultimate 'best friend token'. He created the cover, I created the story.

One thing led to another and Ilan in his excitement told more and more people, we spoke about it more and more and it organically turned into something that would become public and not just between us.

So yes, I may have written a story but Ilan's imagination and talent was definitely my muse when it came to achieving a life long dream.

Taken from Blog entry 'I've written a book!'
Torathena.com

PEEKABOO

Chapter 1.

Jessica had always loved the circus. The performers, the costumes, but mainly, she loved the whole experience just to be close to the animals. Living in Shrewsbury with its meagre 64,000 population had many positives but also contained an equal amount of negatives. Not being close to the sea or any form of zoo was one of those negatives. So whenever Jessica had the opportunity to be around animals that she usually could only ever see on the television, she would grow so excited she wouldn't be able to eat all day leading up to the anticipated event.

August 17th 1996 was one of those magical days when Jessica felt like nothing could go wrong. The travelling circus had arrived and pitched their tent earlier this week, and all Jess could do was harass and beg her parents to take her. Eventually they caved into her desperate pleas and decided to take her as her 7th birthday present.

Jess was an only child to George and Harriet Befria. Very loved but not often spoilt, Jess was as humble as a child knew how to be.

She had imaginary friends to keep her company, would dress in her mum's clothes and pretend she was all grown up while she would play games all day long. Her favourite activity was to simply pretend she was travelling the world, "making poorly animals feel better about themselves." She was far from perfect and would occasionally take advantage of being an only child, knowing her parents did not have to divide their attention between her and her non-existent siblings; but overall, she was well behaved. She understood the meaning of no when her parents would put their foot down and asked for very little. So the fact Jess had written a letter every day explaining why she needed to go to this circus was a clear indication of how much she truly wanted to go.

Wearing her Sunday best, Jess wanted to make a good impression. She had brushed her hair five times more than necessary and even attempted shining her own shoes, which resulted in a filthy and costly stain on the carpet. Today must have been her lucky day, as her parents did not scold her too much. Soon an ecstatic Jess was on her way to her very first circus.

Jess felt completely euphoric as she sat ringside watching the electric performance take over her. Billy Bob's Spectacular Circus was famous across the country, boasting it housed the best performers anyone could possibly dream to see.

The air was thick with excitement. As elephants swayed their heads, the children would look up at them in awe and then scream in delight as the Ringmaster sprayed two acrobats with water and then poured confetti all over them. The aroma inside the tent was a heavy bitter sweet smell of hay, manure and popcorn. The lights constantly flickered off and on, changing colours to fit the mood of each performance, casting long moody shadows across the red and white striped tent. Jess was drunk off the whole experience and she honestly couldn't remember when she had been happier. Maybe she never would be again.

Jess was surprised even further by the fact her parents had bought tickets to go backstage and feed the animals after the show. After overindulging on popcorn and candy floss, all the children were practically vibrating from a sugar high. Each child would quickly run from one animal pen to another, taking in little information, completely unable to focus whilst having so much energy to burn. All but Jessica, who took her time with each animal, learning each of their names and talking to some of the stars of the show, who were clearly uncomfortable with the energetic children around their animal family. During the hustle and bustle, Jess was walking away from the pony she had just been feeding when she saw, at the end of the tent, a clown staring at her. She specifically didn't remember seeing a single clown during the show. In fact, she remembered being heartbroken to discover that this circus advertised there were no clowns. This had upset her greatly, as clowns had always seemed a highlight to any circus, so she became excited to finally see one.

Still in the distance, the clown slowly raised one hand up and waved her over. She looked around to check it was actually herself the clown was addressing. It was. She stepped closer, wanting to go over and say hi, but whenever she seemed to move her foot forward, he would slowly drag his foot away. Forever keeping his distance from her. She started to notice that his costume seemed dirty. His white baggy jumpsuit was more of an off-white colour, almost grey in places. His blue and orange patches seemed faded and torn, one patch was barely attached and hanging limply over itself, flapping against his leg whenever he moved. He was making what looked like a balloon animal. Was it for her? She hadn't noticed him getting a balloon out of any pocket, or even blow it up, but there he was, making the shape of a poodle with a bright blue sausage shaped balloon. She had been so transfixed on him, not taking her eyes off him whilst weaving through the crowd that she hadn't even realised she was no longer in the same room anymore. She was suddenly alone in what looked like a walk-in supply cupboard. There was metal shelving lining the walls with different shaped boxes filling them. There was only one solitary beam of light coming from what appeared to be a small tear in the roof of the tent, so it was too dark to tell what any of these items were. Not daring to move any further into the room she stood looking around but could not see the clown anywhere. She also could not see the entrance and was suddenly growing anxious at how her memory could not recall walking in here. All of a sudden she could hear shuffling. Straining her eyes, she could just about see on the other side of the room a dark figure moving slowly towards her. She called out to it but they didn't reply. Using the little light she had, she could roughly work out that this was the clown she had been following but now, unlike before, he was moving closer to her. His hands masked his face as he shuffled his way towards her gradually. Even in the darkness, Jess noticed shapes on the back of the clown's hands but he was not yet close enough for the marks to be clear.

As the distance grew shorter, she could identity the shapes as comically drawn eyes, staring back at her on the back of his hand. They made her feel uneasy as he approached, getting closer until he was just a dark silhouetted figure towering over Jess.

He slowly and silently knelt down to her level. He stayed there almost frozen, with these drawn eyes gazing back, mute. For a moment she stopped worrying about how she got there and concentrated on the more pressing matter of who this person was.

She reached out her hand slowly towards his face and touched the cartoon eyes. Suddenly, she felt tremendous pain shoot down her arm. Paralysed in agony and fear, the room did not seem so dark anymore and she could clearly see the clown jolt away from her touch, removing his hands from over his eyes to reveal half a clown face, half a melting, grotesque scar. One side of his head was smoking and golden embers flickered around his wounds like glitter. The smell of burning hair suddenly surrounded her and filled her nostrils to the point she almost threw up. His skin peeled away, revealing a shining cheekbone as he looked directly at her. His mouth opened to speak but all she could hear was her own screams.

Chapter 2

"Miss Jessica!"

"It's Miss Befria. Jessica is my first name."

"Miss Beefy-er, why do we have to stay inside today? It's not fair!"

"Because Emily, it's raining. If I let the class go out to play and you get ill, I will have all your parents come to shout at me. Is that what you want?"

"I won't get ill, I promise!"

Jess knew this conversation was going nowhere, so she patted Emily softly on the back whilst simultaneously nudging her towards the painting area she had set up. Being a teacher was not easy at the best of times; but looking after a classroom full of seven year old children who just want to go out and play when they cannot, was a particularly testing experience for her. Jess was 27 now, a teacher with two years' experience under her belt and currently had not given into her loneliness at home by buying five cats.

"Miss Befria, could I speak to you for a minute?" The sharply dressed teacher of Class 1 and also Jess's best friend was standing in the doorway. The children giggled and made taunting noises, thinking the only reason a teacher ever wanted to talk to anyone was because they were in trouble. Ignoring the children she walked straight to the door, reminding herself she chose this profession.

"Everything ok Dee?" Jess whispered so the first names went undetected by the children.

"I'm pregnant."

"WHAT!?" The children jumped on the spot and then started to shift uncomfortably at the sudden outburst from a teacher.

"I'm joking." Dee laughed, more to herself than anyone else. The children, seeing the adults laugh became relaxed again and continued their chosen activities. "I'm just bored. However, have you seen the new guy? I wouldn't mind reproducing with him."

"I can't believe anyone allows you near children," Jess sighed.

"I know, it's brilliant. I better get back. I think I left the scissor draw unlocked." Dee winked at her friend, giggled and strutted off down the hall in impossibly tall but equally stunning black heels.

Jess constantly questioned if Dee acted the way she did purely to get a rise out of her timid friend.

"She wouldn't really forget to lock the scissor drawer, surely?" she wondered. Her and Dee were completely opposite people but they would joke about how that made them such good friends. Dee constantly dressed smarter than she needed to for any occasion and always appreciated the finer things in life. She had only moved to the tiny village of Beverley, East Yorkshire because her mum lived there and became very ill and needed someone to take care of her. Dee was honest, blunt and often offended people because of it. However, she wasn't cold and genuinely cared for the people around her. She moved from London only a month before Jess arrived and feeling both outsiders to such a tightly knitted community, they instantly bonded. Two years later, they were an unbreakable odd couple. However, pretending to be pregnant, even for a minute, was a new line for her to cross.

She had not met the new teacher yet and was in no rush to do so either. It was just another colleague for her to work with and she couldn't understand why all the teachers were acting like it was a new national holiday. She had gone into the teacher's lounge this morning before class had started and all she could hear were the teachers, especially the female ones, gossiping away like they belonged on the playground instead of the children. Granted, nothing new or exciting happened in Beverley. It was even smaller than where she grew up. She suspected she might be the only person living there that actually appreciated the quiet and mundane life that she lived.

Jess survived the remainder of the day the same way she always did. In a series of blurry moments, praying, rewarding and scolding. It was a fine balancing act; she often thought of it like people who spin those plates on sticks. You had to keep your eye on every plate, or you would probably lose momentum and smash everything. For her, the children were the plates. She adored looking after her Year 2 class, but a hoard of seven year olds who just want to play can easily exhaust anyone after six hours. The children were finally leaving, all alive and healthy, and Jess took this as another victory. All that was left now was cleaning up after hours of mild, organised chaos. She straightened the chairs, tidied the colouring pencils, put miscellaneous school ties, hairpins and even a sock into a lost and found box, as some parents would surely come back to reclaim what their hard-earned wages had purchased for their careless children. This job was hard, but rewarding. She loved being around the children before reality broke them of their carefree spirit. She missed those days of not even having to think of what would happen the next day, let alone planning mortgages, classes and everything in between. She hadn't felt truly free from worries since -

"Hi, sorry, I didn't mean to make you jump Miss Befria." The head teacher had knocked on the door, startling Jess and waking her from her own thoughts.

"Oh, not at all Mrs Hall. I'm sorry, I was in my own world." Mrs Hall was a stern, middle aged lady who had a grey bun so tight on her head it looked like she was trying to give herself a facelift. Her thin 5ft 3in frame was never to be mistaken for weak. She took her job very seriously, and even when not in the presence of the children, she preferred all the teachers refer to each other by their surnames. It seemed more professional that way, and to Mrs Hall being professional was the most important part of any job.

"It's quite alright, I just wanted to bring by Mr Healy, our new Year 6 teacher. I don't think you two have been introduced yet, have you? Mr Healy, this is Miss Befria who runs Year 2."

Jess leaned over and shook his hand, smiling politely. Matt was incredibly handsome but Jess became increasingly aware he was staring at her shoulder. She tried to subtly inspect the target area and realised that she had at some point got paint in her long, mousy brown hair, which had now become a tangled and knotted mess.

"Well, now, Miss Befria was the last stop of this tour," Mrs Hall concluded. "So you are free of me for now. I am sure you will fit right in here, but if you need anything, please don't hesitate to ask." The headmistress then shook his hand and walked out with such a regal air about her you would think she was the queen of England. It was obvious Mrs Hall saw this school as a stepping stone towards her grand ambition of the Headmistress job at Beverley Grammar School. Running the oldest state school in England had an appeal no other could offer.

The moment Mrs Hall was out of earshot, Jess smiled warmly at Matt. "You don't have to call me by my surname, that's just something she insists on. My name is Jess."

"Yeah, that's unusual I have to admit. I'm Matt." He was incredibly attractive. Tall, slightly tanned with a physique that made her think he went to the gym a lot more than she did. His clothes were smart, but he was wearing jeans and a shirt, not a suit like every other man who worked here. His slightly long hair had evidentially been brushed and tied back to be tamed at some point earlier on, but stray strands had escaped, making him look like those models who spend hours to get the 'just out of bed' look. Jess realised she had been staring far too intently at him, blushed and returned to cleaning up.

"Mrs Hall is quite a character, but she is very good at her job," Jess rambled on. "How have you found your first day then?"

"It was fun."

"Fun?"

"Yes, your children have a lot of energy to burn, keeps me on my toes."

"Prepare for your toes to get sore very quickly," Jess teased.

"Yeah?" Matt had started to help her tidy up and the movement seemed to ease Jess.

"Just like you said. They have a lot of energy, I think it's something we must put in our water!" she joked.

"I think they're just kids. Do you not remember being a kid and having so much energy you could play for hours without a coffee break?"

"Not really," Jess admitted.

"Well, maybe you were just lazy." Jess felt offended by this statement; for some stranger to make such a harsh judgement on someone he had only just met. She looked up to respond but saw him standing there smiling at her, showing off a predictable set of perfect teeth. Berating herself on how sensitive and foolish she was being, she forced out a weak laugh.

"Yeah, maybe. So what brings you here? You sound southern."

"You are correct. I have only just passed my PGSE, I had no ties where I was living and took the first job that accepted me really. Nothing special I'm afraid."

They continued to tidy up saying nothing, only breaking the silence when he wasn't sure where something would go. Jess felt so awkward and was very grateful there was very little left to do. She turned off all the lights, closed the door behind her and they walked uncomfortably down the corridor together.

"Befria? That's an unusual name."

"It's Swedish."

"You're Swedish?"

"I suppose one of my ancestors was, but it isn't something I have ever looked up. I know it means to set free, or liberator... or something like that."

"Have you ever liberated anyone?"

"At least one child gets stuck in something on a daily basis. I guess I was destined for this job." The mood lightened between them with every step away from that classroom, which would forever be home to that awkward first encounter.

By the time they had reached the carpark they were laughing and joking like they had worked together for years. Their mood was only dampened by the fact it was raining heavier than ever.

"Well this is my car," Jess announced a little too formally. She looked around and noticed that there were no other cars. "Did you not drive here?"

"Er... no, I underestimated the weather today and wasn't sure how busy the carpark would be."

"Do you need a lift?" Jess offered.

"No, don't be silly, you don't even know where I live, I could be miles away from you," he protested.

"Call it a welcome present. I couldn't allow you to go home in this rain."

Matt looked around uncomfortably. It was clear he was torn between walking home in a potential thunder storm, getting in the car with a strange lady or, worst yet, being an imposition. The most British faux pas.

"I promise, I had nothing planned tonight. It will give me something to do if anything," she coaxed. Although she had wished she hadn't made it clear just how available and boring her schedule was. He seemed to shuffle his feet without actually moving anywhere, almost like he was dancing on the spot. Then he suddenly smiled, nodded and they both jumped into the car, grateful for the shelter away from such a heavy downpour.

Jess's good deed was rewarded by discovering Matt didn't live too far from her at all. It was about a 20 minute drive from the school, 40 minutes in this weather.

"You're a very *safe* driver."

"What is that meant to mean?" Jess scoffed.

"You're going 20mph."

"It's raining, you should always drive slower when the roads are wet."

"Slower, yes, but it's a 40mph limit here," he jeered.

"It's better to be cautious than be dead."

"Are you always cautious?"

"When driving?"

"Anytime," he enquired.

"I'm not an adrenaline junkie, if that's what you mean." Jess had her eyes glued to the road but she could sense Matt staring at her. She felt like his eyes would burn a hole through her if he held his gaze any longer. It was not what he had meant, but she was not about to open up about her safe little existence to someone she had barely known an hour.

"One day Jess, you will realise, the biggest thing you will regret, is not doing what you could have done, but didn't do," Matt preached.

"My, my, aren't we the insightful one? Well if you're quite done playing Doctor Phil, I'd like to ask you some things," Jess teased.

"Shoot, what do you want to -"

Before Matt could finish that sentence the car tyres were screeching; the car was turning too quickly and for what felt like forever they were driving on the wrong side of the road before Jess could regain control of the car and steady it again.

"What just happened, did we hit something?!" Matt shouted.

"I am so sorry. I thought I saw something back there. Are you ok?"

"No, yeah, sorry I'm fine. Good job you do drive slower than snails," Matt said, relaxing, the danger having passed. Jess tried to laugh but only managed a meek choking noise, unaware her knuckles were turning white on the steering wheel.

They barely spoke a word on the way back. Every time Matt would try to talk to her, he would be lucky to get even a single word response. He had already had the notion that she may be a nervous driver and a possible collision would be enough to rattle anyone, so he didn't push conversation. They made it to his address unscathed and silent.

"I haven't finished unpacking yet, but you're more than welcome to come in for tea or coffee if you're still too shaken to drive?" he offered.

"Thank you so much, but seriously I'm fine. Like I said, I just thought I saw something."

He nodded, left the car, and walked up to his home. Exhaling deeply, she drove back to her house. Without incident, she parked in front of her house, grabbed her things, got out, locked the car, walked up to her door, went inside and closed it behind her, making sure it was firmly locked. She stood there, surveying her small, pristine living space, and crumbled to the floor. Leaning against the door with her knees against her chest she desperately tried to slow down her breathing. She tried to tell herself that she was ok and that she was safe now.

She knew she had seen something.

She *knew* she had seen someone dressed like a clown standing at the side of the road with his hands over his face; with cartoon eyes staring back at her.

Chapter 3

Entering the staff room, Jess could instantly sense the excitement in the room. The teachers were talking and giggling instead of avoiding each other whilst trying to get their first fix of coffee in the morning.

"Yeah, he is cute isn't he."

"Why would he move here?" Dee asked Sarah, the Year 4 teacher.

"Who knows, maybe he has family here, has anyone asked?"

"He's not that good looking," mumbled a male teacher walking past.

"Oh, is Greg jealous that he may have competition?" Dee jeered at the sulking teacher. "Oh hey Jess, you ok?"

Jess suddenly realised she had been stood there staring at them open mouthed and glassy eyed since she had walked into the teacher's lounge. "Oh yeah, sorry Dee, just spaced out a little, haven't had my morning coffee yet," Jess lied as she refilled her cup for the second time that morning.

"Sarah and I were just talking about the new boy. Have you met him yet?" Dee asked in an unnaturally high pitched voice she put on when trying to get information out of people. She walked over from the seating area and rested her hands on the kitchen counter next to Jess. Dee stood out even more when stood next to Jess, with her short bright blonde hair, her expensive suits that made her look more like a lawyer than a teacher and her heels that got husbands in trouble with their wives at parents' evening. Jess never wore anything sharp or expensive. Her hair was brushed today, and that was as good as it got. She wore plain black trousers, with a light blue blouse and a slightly worn, but simple black cardigan. Not to mention a pair of flat black shoes. When she did brave heels, they were never taller than an inch.

Jess took her time pouring the hot water into the coffee-stained mug she always used. She stirred the spoon, held the mug in both hands and turned to rest against the cabinet, surveying the only room no children could be in. It was nicknamed The Sanctuary. She shifted her eyes over to see Dee leaning far too close for comfort, eager to discuss her future husband. Jess wasn't looking forward to the reaction she would get when she explained that Matt had been in her car last night, and was debating how much she should tell her.

"So have you met him?!" Dee repeated, getting more high pitched.

"Last night," Jess confirmed, nodding, but not looking at her nosey friend.

"AND!? He's gorgeous isn't he?"

"He's… an attractive young man," Jess answered, choosing her words carefully.

Dee's entire body seemed to deflate.

"ATTRACTIVE YOUNG MAN!? Jess, you're 27. You're not dried up and wrinkly just yet!"

"Unlike you, I am being professional. I work with him; it's wrong to talk about him like this."

Dee started to bounce "Ah, professional," she winked. "I understand, don't want to leave any evidence around for a sexual harassment claim. Good thinking!"

Jess wanted to argue with her, but she knew that would be a much more difficult path to take so early in the morning. Just as she stood there, embracing the silence, Matt walked up to both Jess and Dee. Jess could see in the corner of her eye, Dee trying to stick her hips out more than usual.

"Hey Jess, you ok?" Matt seemed uncomfortable, shifting his eyes between Jess and Dee, who was smiling a little too wide to appear natural.

"Prey always knows when predators are around," Jess thought to herself, sighing at Dee's blatant passes.

"I'm good thanks. Coffee?" She offered, holding up a clean mug from behind her.

"No thank you, I just wanted to make sure you were ok after last night?"

"Yeah, great, no big deal." Jess's manic smile and extra wide eyes - now matching Dee's - blatantly screamed that she was lying. However, it was clear Matt didn't want to talk about this in front of people as he kept shooting confused glances at Dee, who was working her way closer into his personal space.

"Well, as long as you're ok." He shrugged and then nervously turned towards a worn chair in the corner of the room. The moment he sat down and was no longer close enough to hear their conversation, Dee subtly squeezed Jess's arm.

"What happened to professional? Last night? What happened?" Dee's eyes looked hungry for answers. Jess shrugged herself free from the vice grip.

"Absolutely nothing, we were walking out of the school together, it was raining - "

"How romantic," Dee teased.

"It was raining and he didn't have his car with him, so I offered him a ride home."

"That doesn't sound like enough happened for him to ask if you are ok," Dee deduced.

"Oh, the car skidded in the rain slightly." Jess tried to sound as flippant as possible. "You know what I'm like driving, I was a little shaken. I'm over it now."

Dee looked unconvinced, but it was almost 9am and time to head to the classrooms. The truth was, Jess was definitely not over it. She woke up that morning telling herself that nothing was there. She knew what she saw had to be her imagination. She has been working so hard lately and stress can play tricks on an exhausted brain. She knew she was safe; but she did not feel it.

The remainder of the day went by as normal. One of the things about her job that Jess was grateful for, was that the children kept her busy from start to finish. There was no time to dwell on what could or could not have happened. By the time the children had packed up their things and gone home, Jess was starting to feel a little more herself again. She tidied up her class silently and alone, planning everything she needed to get done for tomorrow. She turned off the lights, closed the door and made her way to the main entrance. Walking past the teacher's lounge she could hear noises coming from inside and her heart dropped. She had completely forgotten that there was a staff meeting and she was late; something Mrs Hall never liked in her children or teachers. She inhaled deeply, preparing herself for the judging eyes of her boss as she opened the door.

"Ah! Miss Befria, thank you for joining us. Please, take a seat. We were just going over the new lunch budget and explaining that we now need more supervision during meal times and would like the teachers to take it in turns to help with the lunch ladies."

"Yes, of course Mrs Hall. Sorry I'm late." Jess apologised as she went to the kitchen area and stood there, sheepishly, as all the chairs were now occupied. She looked over at Dee, who was conveniently seated next to Matt and obviously trying to lean in as close as possible to him. Dee shot her a victorious look and Jess couldn't help but admire her best friend's ambition and confidence.

"As I was also saying, Miss Befria," Mrs Hall continued, "we are also going over the school trip taking place this weekend. We will be taking Years 3 and upwards, and need three teachers to accompany them. We have two volunteers, and seeing as you were late I didn't think you would mind being the third."

Jess realised straight away that this was Mrs Hall's punishment for her being tardy. Class trips were not an easy task. The children were hard to manage as they were so excited and it was a truly exhausting ordeal at the best of times. So much could go wrong - more than in a classroom - and you were responsible for anything that happened. She also knew that she was in no place to refuse doing it.

"Of course Mrs Hall. I wasn't aware there was a class trip planned. What is it for?"

"Oh did you not know? The circus arrived last night and we thought we could all take them before it packs up and leaves again."

Jess could not move. She felt paralysed. She wanted to scream, outright object, run, but nothing happened. All of a sudden she seemed acutely aware of everything in the room. The smell of instant coffee, the stale smell of smoke clinging to the teacher next to her. She could hear someone scratching their beard across the room from her, and Matt. She noticed how Matt was looking at her. He seemed intrigued. No, concerned. She then noticed Dee had the same expression, in fact, the whole room did. She suddenly felt on display to everyone and wondered why.

"Are you ok Miss Befria?" Mrs Hall inquired.

"No."

"No?"

"I mean yes, sorry. The circus. You want me to go to the circus," Jess confirmed, shaking her head clear.

"I want you to escort the children to the circus, yes. It's not the worst job I've handed out to staff. You will be fine. At least you get a day off work." Mrs Hall turned away from her and continued talking about parent's evening coming up. The matter had been closed and Jess was going to the circus.

When the meeting was done Jess shuffled out silently. Dee ran up behind her and followed her out of the building.

"What was that about?" Dee asked.

"What do you mean?"

"Did you see yourself in there? When that crank told you that you had to go to the circus you looked like she had ordered you to kill your family."

"I did?"

"Jess, you went so white I thought you may have died standing up."

"Well, that explains why everyone was looking at me," Jess thought to herself.

"I'm fine."

"You didn't look it. Why aren't you telling me the truth?"

"I just don't like the circus."

"That's it? That's why you looked like you were about to throw up?"

"It's hard to explain." She knew her friend would never be satisfied with any answer she gave. "I am not good around clowns."

"Oh who is?!" Dee laughed, placing her hand on Jess's arm. "They are creepy, but it's ok and do you know why? Because I was one of the volunteers."

"You? You have never volunteered for any of the trips since I've known you." Jess stared at Dee, who was staring back with the most exaggerated innocent expression on her face.

"Matt was the first to volunteer. I don't know if he is a genuine saint or if he's just trying to make a good impression in his new job, but I naturally had to show him that I was equally a good person too."

"You're terrifying to the male gender." Jess was grateful that talking about Matt had distracted Dee enough to stop probing.

"I really am. Not as terrifying as a circus is to you though," she teased.

"Oh, we're back on that again." Jess started to walk away again, back to her car, and Dee followed quickly behind.

"I just don't understand. Did something happen? Did you get stuck in a little clown car? Or did an elephant nearly squish you?" Dee pushed.

"A clown scared me when I was seven. Apparently I was really traumatised from it for a long time. I haven't really liked anything to do with a circus since." Jess made a conscious effort to make her voice sound as casual as possible.

"Oh you don't need to worry then," Dee brightened. "This circus actually advertises no clowns."

Jess froze. Ice seemed to pump through her veins.

"What circus is in town? Do you know what it is called?"

"Yes, it's, err, Billy Bob's Spectacular Circus."

Chapter 4.

Jess lay in bed with the lights on, staring at the ceiling. The clock on the bedside table confirmed she should have been asleep hours ago, but the ability to fall into a slumber was momentarily impossible.

Today had forced her to think about a memory she spent her life trying to forget. Jess never remembered how she escaped from the burning clown at the circus. Her father said he had already been looking for her as she had been out of his sight for a long time and when he heard a scream from behind a closed door, he recognised it and came and found his daughter, on the floor, crying and hysterical. No one believed the tale she told, they all thought it was the product of an overactive imagination. The only evidence she had at the time were burn marks on the tips of her fingers on her right hand.

She tried to rationalise that the memories of a seven year old could not be trusted. That she had been so excited and impressionable that she would have believed anything. The reality was, though, she still believed her seven year old self more than the empty words that people were feeding her right now.

"It was just a trick someone was playing on you."

"They don't even have any clowns at that circus."

"Why did you follow a stranger anyway!?"

"It happened years ago, get over it."

The worst part of the whole experience was not the ordeal itself but how everyone around her reacted. Through fear and ignorance, the people close to her in her life did not protect her or care for her, but berated and scolded her. No one believed her, she was alone from the age of seven to deal with her own fears and emotions. Years later she could remember how the clown's burns still shimmered and how the smell of burning skin and hair clogged up her nose, and it would be all she could smell for days. She remembered every moment so clearly but constantly questioned if it was real, no matter how ingrained it was into her memory.

She continued to toss and turn in her bed, jumping slightly at the slightest sound she could hear. She lived alone with no pets so couldn't blame any noise on them. Jess knew she was too fussy and particular about so many things that a housemate would drive her insane and a pet would ruin everything. Her bedroom for example was all white and cream. Her large double bed was covered in white cotton sheets, with white fluffy pillows of many different shapes. Opposite the bed was a tall white dresser with a mirror and a few cosmetic items neatly placed beside it. To her left was a tall window that overlooked the neighbourhood and a small front garden and drive. She had soft, transparent white netted curtains covering the windows, allowing light to still come through but giving her added privacy. She also had an extra set of long heavy, thick white curtains over that; these were more for show than anything and were very rarely closed completely. To her right was the bedroom door leading into an equally immaculate and pastel house. She took pride that her house was show room ready at all times.

Eventually she fell asleep but it was a restless experience. She dreamed of bright colours, loud music and could even smell the bittersweet aroma of hay, manure and fresh popcorn. She was standing at the side of the road where a circus was pitched. Not just any circus, but Billy Bob's Spectacular Circus. She couldn't see a sign anywhere confirming this, but she knew without question; the way you always seem to know these things when dreaming. There were people running about getting tickets, parents trying to hold their children's excited hands, boys buying candy floss for their dates. Everyone seemed happy. She stepped forward towards the circus and every time she moved, everyone blurred past her in slow motion. Sound would distort slightly as if she was listening to everything whilst submerged underwater. The people weren't dressed in modern clothes but from a couple of decades previous. With every step towards the circus, the lights from inside the big top would go dimmer. Only by the time she reached the entrance to the circus did she realise that she was the only person there and all the lights were completely turned off. As she stood there, questioning what to do, she could see her own breath in the air by the light of the moon and she could feel the cold air tingle on her skin.

She started to follow the big top around. Around the first corner she could see the caravans parked up beside the tent. All were dark and silent except for one. She crept towards the vehicle and stepped on to the mini wooden steps leading up to the door.

She could hear music...

She couldn't recognise it but it made her blood run cold. As she stood, rooted to the spot, she could hear more than just the music from inside the caravan;

She could hear crying...

Wanting to run but as if acting on instinct she went to knock on the door to check if the person crying was ok.

Frozen in terror, her hand never made it to the door. She heard shuffling from behind her but it was the smell that stopped her in her tracks. As if on autopilot she slowly turned around. The smell of burning hair and melting flesh was so intense she was sure she could taste it. Her eyes watered from the rancid smell and her throat went tight from wanting to gag. She knew what was waiting for her, she could not stop turning, she could not run. She turned to face those cartoon eyes staring back at her.

Jess woke up wrestling the blanket, terrified, screaming and covered in sweat. The air could not reach her lungs and she couldn't see anything but black. She blindly stretched her hand out to the side of the bed looking for the lamp. Switching it on, the room went from black to a warm and soothing yellow as the bulb warmed up. As the bulb got brighter, Jess felt more safe. It took several minutes to fully calm down and realise that what she had just experienced was nothing but a dream.

It haunted her just how lucid that dream was. She was convinced she could still smell the popcorn. The night air had pierced her lungs and the fear she felt when she saw those cartoon eyes had still not completely left her system. She turned to check the time. The clock read 3:05 am. It was going to be a long night.

Chapter 5

"Damn, Jess, you look like crap."

"Thanks Dee. Can always count on you to cheer me up whenever I'm low," Jess mocked as she stirred her morning coffee, leaning back on the counter as she did every day during her morning routine. She caressed her stained mug with both hands and sipped slowly, wondering, if she wished hard enough, would this burnt instant coffee magically turn into a beautiful latte. Or Scotch.

The warmth from the cup was welcome as she looked around, watching all the other teachers carry out their own morning rituals. Most involved solitude whilst they ate up the last few minutes of quiet from their day. All involved caffeine. After her nightmare last night, Jess had found it impossible to go back to sleep and she knew she was going to need a lot more than just one cup this morning. Today was not going to be an easy one to get through.

"Are you ill?" Dee asked, looking concerned at the dark circles under her best friend's eyes.

"No, I didn't sleep very well, that's all. Plus, I need to speak to Mrs Hall and I'm not looking forward to that."

"Why?"

"I can't go on that school trip Dee, I just can't."

"No, Jess, you can't go to Grace and say you can't do your job because the circus gives you goosebumps."

"Mrs Hall," Jess corrected.

"Oh bugger Mrs Hall, she isn't even in this room for god's sake. We're not seven years old, no matter how much she likes to treat us like it."

Jess hated to admit it, but Dee had a point. She knew, in reality, if she went to her employer and explained that she couldn't take the children on a school trip because she believed a clown that only she could see had tried to hurt her 20 years ago, she would be laughed out of the office. She also worried that she would then be monitored closely under the belief that maybe she wasn't even stable enough to teach children; one wrong move and she could be out of her job. She had very little savings and would find herself in trouble very quickly. All that trouble, for speaking the truth. The reality hit her much harder than her cup of coffee that morning. Jess had to go to the circus.

For October the weather was actually beautiful and the children were taking full advantage of being able to play outside whilst the sun was shining. Jess was fortunate enough not to be helping out on dinner duty today but she also felt she would not enjoy the company of the staff room right now. She had been sitting on the window ledge in her own classroom watching the children run around the playground, carefree and happy. She envied every gleeful moment the children naively laughed away. She held her uneaten sandwich, willing herself to try and develop some sort of appetite.

"Hey Jess." She turned around to see Matt in the doorway. She had not heard him approach but strangely, considering her state of mind, also did not jump when he spoke. She had been so deep in her own thoughts she had no time to react. Then she worried why Matt would even be there. She had been so tired she considered that she may have actually had dinner duty today and completely forgotten, which was the last thing she needed since forgetting the staff meeting the day before.

"Hey, you ok? I haven't forgotten anything have I?" Jess enquired, trying to stay calm and innocent.

"No, I just, you seemed quiet this morning, I just thought I would check if you were ok."

Matt edged into the room. He knew this was Jess's room and did not want to impose, but also did not want to stand awkwardly at the door.

"Oh! *Seemed quiet* must actually mean *looked like crap*," Jess teased. "I'm fine, I'm just exhausted, I barely slept last night. I'm lucky to be standing if I'm honest."

"Anything I can help with?" he asked, edging further into the room.

"Not unless you have a clone who will go to the circus instead of me?" Matt shot a puzzled look and Jess, realising what she had said and not really wanting to explain any further, shrugged her shoulders. "Haha, ignore me." She finally looked directly at Matt and shot him the meekest, but genuine smile. She noticed how

Matt was now wearing trousers and wondered if Mrs Hall had given her passive aggressive speech of *clothing dignity* yet, or if Matt was just trying to fit in more with what everyone else would wear. His not so tamed hair, once again trying to break free from the ponytail, gave hope to his 'bad boy' image.

"Dee told me you hate the circus."

"Of course she did," she stated. Jess was too exhausted to react but if she could have, she would already be halfway down the hall about to give her best friend a piece of her mind.

"Yeah, she told me this morning. Your friend really likes to talk," Matt confessed. Jess laughed to herself. Dee was always the life of the party but she had noticed Dee became an increased extrovert around Matt.

"Yeah, she's a social butterfly alright," she mumbled.

"Do you want to talk about it?"

"About what?"

"She said a clown scared you."

"It did." She was too tired to lie. Matt stood still in the middle of the classroom, completely at a loss with what he should do. He was only a few feet away from her but it felt like he was standing, vulnerable in a wide clear opening whilst predators surrounded him unseen in the foliage. There was always an awkward tension between them whenever they were in this room, it would seem.

"Then why are you going?"

"Because," Jess exhaled, "I don't want Mrs Hall to think I'm weak, lazy, a liar or crazy and then fire me."

"She is not going to fire you for not wanting to take the children on a school trip. Dee and I were the only ones to volunteer. *Nobody* wants to go."

She just stared at him, it was so endearing that he was trying. It was more than what most people did and this was only the third day they had been in each other's lives. However, he didn't truly know what had happened. If he listened to her explain the whole story, he would think she was crazy too, she knew it.

"I won't lie Jess, I would love for you to accompany me to the circus, but if you really don't want to go and you don't want to ask Grace, I will ask around with the other teachers and use my *new guy* charm and ask if any of them will swap with you."

She wanted to cry with gratitude but she also didn't have much hope for the outcome being in her favour.

"Thank you."

He looked at her so intently she blushed, unsure if her response had offended him, but he eventually smiled, almost to himself, and walked out. Like all people who would describe themselves as broken, she struggled to trust people, but for some reason she trusted Matt after only knowing him a few days. She saw him as naive but genuinely decent. She just did not fully understand why his interest would be so invested in the bland character that was Jess. She knew she wasn't adventurous, she had never even dyed her hair from the natural mouse brown she was born with. No crazy hair styles or fashion disasters had ever been experienced either. Long straight hair hung around her plain, minimal makeup applied face whilst wearing only office trousers and plain shirts in work, or the same comfortable jeans accompanied with non-inspiring pastel t-shirt when at home. Dee was desperate to give her a makeover but Jess had always told everyone, and herself, she was happy with who she was.

Alone with her thoughts again, she turned her direction from the empty doorway back to the window to look outside towards the playground. That's when she saw it. Almost falling off the ledge and practically forcing her face through the glass to get a closer look, she could see something crouched down, with its back to her in the corner of the field. It was hunched over but she could see the grey rags with a couple of torn blue patches and puffs of blue hair protruding from his head. It looked like a clown. She struggled to breathe. All she could hear was a ringing in her ears whilst her legs forgot how to move.

It can't be...

She knew it could not be what she had seen when she was seven, she would never know the truth about that day, but it could not be happening now. Losing all control of her actions she found herself walking straight out of her class, locked the door behind her and headed straight towards the field. Children were running around her playing, they did not seem to notice or care about the figure crouching in the far corner. As she got closer she could see the dirty rags that were once a white patchwork jump suit. She could see the puffs of blue frizzy hair more closely. She could also smell a faint aroma of burning hair even from here. Half way across the field a young child tugged on her sleeve.

"Miss, miss what is that?" The young child asked, pointing towards where the clown was crouched.

"Nothing John, but can you stay off the field please whilst I double check." She quickly turned to check the expression on the child's face. It was cautious but calm with the presence of a teacher. The child nodded and walked off the grass, grumbling to himself whilst he kicked a pebble away from him. Jess turned back to approach the corner but let out a little whimper, because whatever was in that corner was no longer there. She frantically looked around but it was gone. She eyed the playground, searching for a teacher. She saw Mrs Douglas standing there on duty talking to two girls fighting over a doll. She walked straight over and interrupted the girls without apologising.

"Did you see anyone enter the school yard today? Just now?"

"No Miss Befria. Should I have? Is someone here?"

"Did you see anything over there?" Jess questioned, pointing towards the corner in the field.

"No, nothing, I've been out the whole dinner period and I haven't seen anyone but you or the children, are you ok?"

Jess could not stop looking around. The world was spinning around her and nothing was making sense.

"I'm fine," she lied. Jess walked off without saying another word, questioning her own sanity.

"Maybe I didn't see anything. No I must have, John saw it too. Maybe he was pointing at something else. He didn't specifically say he had seen a clown. Did I see a clown? Our eyes only take in so much and our brains make up the rest. But I smelt something. That could have been from a nearby house burning something and you

mistook it for what you think it was." She rambled on incessantly like that in her head, trying to rationalise everything she thought she had just seen.

Jess was questioning her very sanity by the time she approached her classroom again. Not trusting her eyes, nose or memory, she decided that she must be seeing things through complete exhaustion. Unlocking the classroom door she went to enter her sanctuary, but instantly she could tell that something was wrong. As she was opening the door, she could have sworn she saw something run past. Something large, dirty with tufts of blue, that could no longer be seen anywhere in the room. The smell of burning hair consumed her from the moment she stepped through the doorway and the room felt so warm that she began to sweat uncontrollably. She was about to conclude that was she actually going crazy when she looked at the blackboard. She quickly caught her scream by placing a hand over her mouth. With tear-filled eyes she stared in horror. Quickly scribbled onto the board was the word *Peekaboo*.

Chapter 6

Jess burst into the teacher's lounge. The room was full of desperate teachers making the most of their precious lunch break. Her eyes darted about, searching each person until she saw Dee, who was in the corner reading a gossip magazine, a self-confessed guilty pleasure of hers. With her eyes fixated on her friend, she stormed across the room, paying no attention to her surroundings and almost fell over a chair she did not see.

"Jess, what's the rush?" Dee laughed, barely looking up enough to identify her friend.

"Have you been in my classroom today?" The words fell out her mouth faster than she could breathe.

"What?"

"Please, have you?" Jess pleaded.

"No. Why? Has something been taken? Jess, you're shaking." Dee was looking at Jess now, but still holding the magazine high up to glance at.

"Promise me, you wouldn't lie to me about this would you?"

"Jess, honest, I haven't, what's up?" Dee moved her entire attention on to her friend now, put the magazine down and stood up, holding both of her friend's hands in her own.

Jess did not react to the sincere act of concern. Without saying a word she looked around for the other suspect but Matt was not there. She darted out of the room, leaving Dee utterly in shock as she watched her friend leave. Jess made her way to the Year 6's classroom, grabbing hold of the walls every now and again whenever she felt another fainting spell attack. She finally made it to his room, where he was sitting behind his desk. She walked straight inside without waiting for an invitation.

"Hey Jess, you ok?"

"Have you been in my classroom today?"

"What? You know I have."

"When?" She wanted to cry. She believed he was about to confess to the blackboard, probably try to laugh it off as a harmless prank. She would never forgive him, she had totally thought he was someone better than that.

"When I was talking to you?" Matt looked as confused as Dee. The expression was clear that he knew nothing of the terror written on her blackboard. She felt like a fool to instantly jump to conclusions, to assume he could be so cruel. It was humiliating to forget only twenty minutes ago, they were talking by her window but she had to push past that, she had to be completely sure.

"No. I mean after that. Did you go back?"

"No, I kind of got the feeling you wanted to be alone. Is something up?"

"Yes, no. I don't know." Tears started to form in the corners of her eyes again. Matt stood up and faced her, gently holding her arms. Jess found it odd that people needed to be at equal heights and touching when caring for someone in need.

"What's happened?"

"Someone was in my room," she explained, looking at the floor. It wasn't a lie and she knew it would have been someone she knew who did it, but she still felt her cheeks flush and the hair on her arms tingle thinking about it.

"How do you know?"

"They wrote something on the board."

"What did they write?" Matt asked. Jess couldn't remove her eyes from the floor, being held and listened to was comforting her but as she was calming down, she realised how insane the next part would sound if she said what she wanted to say. "Jess, what did it say?" Matt pressed.

"Peekaboo."

"Peekaboo?" Matt's grip loosened momentarily on her arm. He did not understand the gravity of the situation that she obviously felt.

"My door was locked." Defeated, Jess realised none of this made sense to anyone but her.

"It's ok, I understand you're on edge right now, but you know kids, someone was probably dared to write something on your board."

"But my door was locked," she repeated.

"Maybe it was unlocked for a moment, maybe the caretaker had to pop in, maybe the caretaker wrote it as a joke, it could mean anything Jess."

Jess felt so ashamed. For a moment she had truly questioned if her friends, knowing how

63

upset she had been, were trying to scare her even more. She hadn't fully understood why that word had been written, it meant nothing to her. All she knew at this moment was that the culprit was not the people she trusted, or was beginning to trust.

"I'm sorry," she whispered.

"For what?"

"Thinking it was you." It was the first time she had raised her head and looked him straight in his eyes, and she was now more scared by the fact that his intense stare made her knees feel slightly weak.

"Don't worry about it." He smiled. "No one is here to hurt you. I'll bet you any money, that some kid had been dared to do it and as we speak, there is a group of kids, scrambling about, laughing at how they have just pulled of their equivalent of a master heist." They both chuckled weakly and then stood there, silent, still looking at each other. The hair on Jess's arms began to tingle again, but this time not because she was scared.

"You're right. I'm just being very sensitive right now." Jess sighed, regaining her cool. She noticed that Matt was still holding on to her arms. She looked down at them and blushed.

"Sorry," he mumbled, removing them, and Jess couldn't help but wonder if she had noticed him slightly blushing himself.

"It's fine, next time I'm that hysterical, grab my arms and then shake me until whatever wire fell loose goes back to place in my brain," she joked, but it was hard to feel completely normal so suddenly. "Lunch will be over soon, I should probably head back."

"If you want to talk later, you know where to find me."

"I know where you work and live now."

"Either place is fine," Matt smirked. Suppressing the explosion of butterflies she just felt in her stomach she nodded coyly and left. She felt such a mixture of emotions right now and utterly drained, but she knew she had to tap into some sort of hidden energy reserve to help her through the remainder of the day. She walked back to her class slowly, concentrating on her breathing with every step. She knew she saw something in the corner of the playground but she couldn't specify what exactly. She knew someone had written something on her board, but she didn't know who. She was starting to question if she was just allowing her childhood scars to haunt her in the present to the point she could be hurting herself. She needed to let it all go and accept whatever her suspicions may be, didn't make them a reality.

Turning a new leaf in her mind, Jess discovered an unknown strength to allow herself to get through the day with not just ease, but pleasure. Focusing on the children, she remembered all over again why she loved this job and even found a moment or two to question what her children with Matt would look like before she would shake her head and scorn such idiotic notions.

After the day was finally over, packing away her supplies she carried herself to the staff room where there was to be a brief staff meeting regarding the parents' evening coming up. For once, Jess was on time and only about half the teachers had already arrived. Jess routinely poured herself a bitter, instant coffee, methodically pouring in the milk and then sugar. Holding her cup in both hands, she turned to lean on the counter to survey the room. She searched through the few people there to see Dee wasn't accounted for yet, so there was no one to interrupt own train of thought whilst quietly staring into her coffee but listening intently at the two women talking across the room.

"Are you going to the circus?"

"Of course! But not with the school, I actually want to enjoy it," the teacher scoffed.

"I know, that new guy asked me to volunteer but I actually can't the day the school is going. I think he was flirting with me, why else would he want me to go with him?"

Hearing those words made a knot form in Jess's stomach, but she refused to analyse it any further.

"What's with the big deal they make over having no clowns?" the first girl asked. "Surely clowns aren't that big a deal?"

Jess felt a disparate kind of knot in her stomach.

"Oh have you not heard? Apparently about 40 years ago, Billy Bob's Spectacular Circus arrived at some town and set up. Whilst there,

67

two children went missing. The police came to investigate and found that the clown had murdered them! The clown wouldn't go down without a fight, and set himself on fire whilst they tried to arrest him and he died!"

"Oh my word, that's awful!" the first woman exclaimed.

"There's more though, depending on what you believe. They say, even though the clown is dead, it doesn't mean he's gone. That he still follows the circus around still trying to claim his next victim."

"Oh, ok! So you were joking about all of this!"

"No it's true! Loads of people all over the country have apparently claimed to have seen him! The circus got a really bad reputation for it, so now they make a point to say they don't have clowns of any type at all! I was reading about it last night!" The two women continued to natter and gossip, one convinced her friend was trying to trick her and the other shrieking louder and louder every time she was declared a liar.

Jess now hadn't moved for a few minutes. She stood there frozen on the spot, nursing a rapidly cooling coffee. Her mind could not stop arguing with itself.

"That's it!" she would think *"That's why I can see the clown and no one else can. It's a ghost! Wait, what? No. Jess, that's beyond stupid."*

Her inward struggle deepened, flitting between belief and judgement, until a third option formed. This was a joke. All the teachers had seen how she reacted to being assigned the job of going to the circus. Maybe they were bored in their own little mundane lives and tried to set a prank of some sort in the playground earlier. Maybe the teachers were speaking obnoxiously loud right now because they *wanted* Jess to hear them. She did not quite understand why she would be the target of such an unprofessional joke, but it certainly made more sense than the idea of a killer ghost coming back for her. Jess looked up from her coffee, scowling at the room. She found it funny how she always felt like she was the outsider in this small town, no one had ever really embraced her except Dee but they all seemed to happily accept Matt with open arms. Confused and belittled, she decided not to care too much about the people in the room. By the time Dee had come to her side, she had already accepted that there was nobody else in this room that she would consider a friend. From now on, she would trust nobody.

Chapter 7

Jess found herself on the side of the road next to a pitched circus. Déjà vu washed over her. Every sound and colour seemed to explode around her, but just like last time, everything seemed blurry. Every step she made towards the circus resulted in her walking through foggy still images, almost as if she was underwater. Every time she moved it was draining, but she kept walking until she stood at the entrance of the big top. Once again, by the time she arrived at the circus doors, all the lights had gone out and no one was around. Time seemed to be moving normally once more as her visible breath steadily swirled around her. She walked around a big top to see a solitary light coming from a caravan. Almost automatically, she approached it, with no thoughts running through her head. She stood, staring up at the door when she realised she could hear crying coming from inside. She was shaking as she clumsily climbed the rickety steps. She had no idea what she was about to encounter. This time she made it to the door and reluctantly looked through a little, mud stained window. Inside, sitting on the floor, trembling, were two children. She stared in absolute horror as she watched a little girl in a blue dress around the age of seven years old, crying, and a boy in a tight brown t-shirt and black shorts of the same age trying to comfort her. Suddenly, she heard a voice from inside from a corner of the caravan she could not see. This was not the voice of a child though, but the voice of a grown man.

"Why are you crying? You don't want to go home yet. Do you want more sweets?" The voice was deep, soothing and calm. He was silent for a moment, Jess imagined him probably trying to show sweets to the children as they both shook their heads. "Why are you still crying?!" The man's voice got louder and more impatient to the point of absolute anger. Suddenly, from a corner of the caravan she could not see, an object flew towards the children, barely missing them. The little girl cried harder and louder, growing more high pitched and hysterical to the point it was beginning to sound like screaming.

This was no longer a dream, but a nightmare. One that felt too real and made Jess feel paralysed with fear. Before she could do anything, a tall figure walked into her line of view. He seemed in his early 20s with thick black hair cut short, but combed back with something greasy as it was so shiny. He was also tall, almost 6ft, strong looking with thick, but not muscular arms and wide shoulders. From a first glance you would say he was attractive.

"Was this the clown out of his costume? Was the clown ever alive? Does that mean he's dead now?" Thoughts wouldn't stop racing through her head until the man reached the point in the room where the children were cowering. He grabbed the crying girl by both shoulders and, with what seemed like ease, picked her up and started to shake her, shouting that she needed to stop crying. This made the little girl scream as loud as she could, and only when the man stopped shaking the child abruptly and turned straight to the door did Jess realise she was screaming too. Seeing that face stare back at her was more haunting than the clown costume itself. He wasn't disfigured, burnt or anything you would class as abnormal. He seemed so ordinary, but with the darkest eyes she had ever seen. From where she stood they looked as black as ink and seemed to drain all hope from Jess's body. His jawline was so sharp and his lips were so thin that it looked like he never laughed. Everything seemed horrifyingly serious. He looked evil.

Before Jess realised what was going on, she was awake again in her own bed. She was sat there, rigid and shaking. Sweat poured out of her as she tried to steady her breathing. Sitting in complete darkness, she questioned what she had just experienced. No dream had ever felt so real. She felt so vulnerable. She constantly reminded herself that it was just a dream. She checked the time... it was only 2am. Worrying that she would no longer be able to get back to sleep, she got up to go and get a glass of water from the kitchen. Suddenly she noticed the smell. She could smell burning. Panicking that she'd left the stove on, she ran downstairs to check everything was okay. Nothing was left on, nothing had been moved. She also realised that the burning could not be smelt in the kitchen, or living room, or anywhere downstairs. She came to the conclusion that she must have left her bedroom window open and the smell was wafting inside from one of the neighbours. She walked back into the kitchen after checking downstairs was safe and secure. She silently poured herself a glass of water and whilst still standing at the sink, drank the whole glass in three large gulps. She poured another glass and walked over to the kitchen table where multiple papers were scattered about over the table in no particular order. After hearing the rumours and gossip of the circus earlier that day she had driven directly home after work and researched as much as she could quickly find, but it wasn't easy. The circus was pretty famous, travelling across the country through three generations but there was little history printed about it. She had finally managed to find a few sites with promising links to people who had actually claimed to have seen the clown itself, but was interrupted by three phone calls. The first one was her weekly phone call off her parents. She had not wanted to worry them and kept the conversation light and pleasant, which accidentally made her come across as rude as she simply didn't have the energy to pretend she was ok. She tried to get them off the phone as quickly as possible without worrying or offending them. The moment that awkward conversation had ended, the phone rang again. This time it had been Dee, who wouldn't let Jess get off the phone until Jess had explained herself about the outburst that had happened at lunch. Reluctantly, Jess did tell her best friend the truth but was disheartened when Dee took Matt's side, saying that it was obviously children. Jess knew that was the rational option but also suspected Dee believed that theory just because Matt did. Eventually, Dee allowed her to end the conversation and hang up. Jess had been more truthful about wanting to get off the phone to her friend. She did not care so much about offending Dee.

Jess still had every intention of continuing her research; it had only been 8pm and there was still plenty of time, but just as she had sat down at the table, fingers poised at the keyboard, the phone rang for the third time. It was Matt, wanting to double check that she was ok. Jess thought that was a sweet gesture but she also did not have time to talk to him either. She planned to speak to him for roughly 10 minutes, like she did to her parents and best friend, then feign tiredness and hang up.

They talked about school at first and what had happened. Jess eventually brushed it off, not wanting to talk about it anymore, so Matt quickly changed the subject to his favourite film, which was Die Hard. After Jess had confessed she had never seen it, he had pretended to hang up in disgust. He made her promise that they would watch it together at Christmas, and this made Jess bite her lip hard to try and stop the smile spreading across her face.

Jess told him about the time she went out for dinner once and ordered steak and the waiter brought out a soup with garlic bread. She was so polite, she sat there and ate the dish she did not even order, and when the bill came, she noticed she was still billed for the steak. Not wanting to cause a fuss, she paid it and left. Matt could not stop laughing down the phone at her.

Then they had spoken about their parents.

"Mine live in London. They moved there because they had some kind of mid-life crisis and wanted to move from somewhere so remote to the bloody capital city," Jess had explained.

"Why didn't you follow them?"

"I'm not a city girl. I think I am the only person who likes the peace."

Matt explained that his parents had emigrated to Spain and now ran a little bar there. From the sounds of it Matt's family seemed quite wealthy; not necessarily rich, but certainly comfortable.

"Why did you bother staying here? You could be living in the sun," Jess asked.

"They live in the Canary Islands, Gran Canaria, to be precise, it's one of the highest places of British emigration in the world. They're just around tourists all the time, nothing is real, everyone on holiday, it's so fake, because they can be."

"So you're not fake?"

"No, I've always hated games, falseness, lies etc. I like real things, real people."

"Do you think I'm real?"

"I think you're the most real person in this town."

"You barely know me," Jess laughed, blushing slightly and smiling uncontrollably.

"This is true," he confirmed, laughing slightly. "But I barely know anyone right now, I've only lived here for two weeks and worked in the school for three days, but I don't play games, I say how I feel. I like how you make me feel when we talk." Jess did not know how to respond to this. She liked him but she had not really thought about it. Her thoughts had been preoccupied by more sinister worries recently.

"I like talking to you too," she confessed.

"Good, then we should do it more often, especially over nicer subjects. Oh man, is that the time, I have a lesson plan I need to finish. I'm glad you're ok Jess, you certainly sound a little better, take care."

Jess had looked at the time to see it was midnight. She had spoken to him for four hours and she could not even recall where the time had gone. It just flew with him, whilst she had tried to rush off the phone from the two most important people in her life. Maybe she liked him more than she had really thought about.

Knowing how late it was, she realised her concentration had vanished and her focus was gone. She gave up the research but left the papers there as a visual reminder to continue it at a later date. She had gone to bed feeling productive and giddy.

Now back in the kitchen, holding her water, fingering through the paper, she told herself now would also not be the best time to be reading up more on what was giving her nightmares. She sleepily climbed her stairs to start her second attempt at a peaceful sleep.

Once in the bedroom she was hit with the unmistakable smell of burning again. Knots formed instantly in her stomach as she recognised this burning smell from her childhood. The more she concentrated on the aroma the more she could smell the usual burning of cloth and material most people may be used to smelling around any generic fire, but the more she inhaled, the unmistakable hint of burning flesh and hair overtook anything else and became the only scent that entered her nose and possessed her senses. Jess reached for the bedroom light by the door, feeling that being able to see everything would protect her, somehow. Her eyes scanned the room frantically for evidence of where the smell had come from, but she could see nothing. She stared across her room, where there was a large window hiding behind heavy curtains, that were drawn shut. She stared at the closed drapes, trying to remember when she had done that. They were always kept half open, whilst she had thinner ones to protect her modesty. Slowly, she edged her way towards the window and, with complete trepidation, threw the curtains back. There was nothing there. She let out a heavy sigh, uncertain what to expect but feeling silly to expect anything at all. After opening the window and closing it again, she determined that the smell was not coming from outside. Resting her hands on the windowsill and staring at the floor, she began to exhale slowly, trying to gather her thoughts. She wanted to tell herself that it was coming from the neighbour's house. Maybe some late-night cooking had gone wrong and because Jess was so tired she had mistaken what the burning was. However, she knew she could not lie to herself about the origin of that unmistakable smell.

Once experienced, it was unforgettable. Suddenly, she realised that the smell was stronger than ever and it was beginning to make her stomach turn. She looked up and froze in horror. She could see in the reflection of the window, a burnt clown standing behind her. She stood there, silent and paralysed, for what felt like eternity. She wondered why he was just standing there, why he would not attack. He stared at her with one round, melting and yellow eye. It looked like the flames were trying to make the eyeball itself pop out, but the drooping socket would just about manage to keep it in place for now. The other eye was not on fire, it remained intense, focused and black. It began to drain all hope away from Jess just by staring into it through a window reflection. Then without warning, he lifted his arm and grabbed hold of hers. The searing pain that flashed through her body at his touch was the most violent thing she had ever experienced. She screamed the second he touched her, but so did the clown. His mouth opened wide. Wider than what should be normal, as it pulled at the melting flesh and blisters. His scream didn't sound human. An echoed screech erupted out of his gaping mouth and it somehow snapped Jess back into reality. She realised she needed to move whilst the clown seemed to be in too much pain to do anything. Jerking her arm away with all her strength, she managed to break free from his grasp. The moment the connection was broken, the pain instantly stopped, but so too did the clown's pain as he had also stopped screaming. He was still within reach from her. His arms reached out to her, but she ducked and moved, knowing that her life would depend on not letting him touch her again. She ran through the open bedroom door, down the stairs, and to the front door. She heard movement upstairs but she had no time to look back or think about what was happening there. She grabbed her keys, unlocked the door, and ran outside. Not stopping for breath she got in her car, started her engine and drove as quickly as she could with no specific direction in mind. Speeding down the road she started to gain some sense. Without slowing down she realised she was going in the direction of Matt's house. It was late, but he was closer than anyone else right now and she had left her phone in the house. She eventually pulled up to Matt's house and pounded on the door until a very tired and confused Matt appeared. His eyes opened wide when he saw the distressed appearance of Jess. Before he could even invite her in she had already run into the house, into his arms shaking; it had been raining all evening and she was wet in her pyjamas.

"Jess. What's happened? Where are your clothes? What's happened? Are you ok?" Only then Jess had realised she was still in her little short Pjs and not even wearing shoes.

"They're at home," she replied, unable to think.

"Why aren't you at home? What's happened?" Matt could feel Jess shaking uncontrollably in his arms, and he held her tight in case it was because she was cold. Jess noticeably started to shake more violently after that question.

"It attacked me," she managed to get out between sobs.

"Who attacked you? Oh my god Jess, we need to call the police." Matt was in a frenzy.

Lack of a good night's sleep and information was making him frantic and high pitched.

"The clown." Jess could feel Matt's body tense up. There was a moment's silence.

"The clown?" His voice had resumed back to its normal tone.

"The clown," Jess confirmed. She was tired of pretending she was normal, she knew what she had seen.

"Jess..." Matt started.

"Just, don't!" Jess broke away from him. She was hysterical. "I know what you're going to say! That it's impossible, I must have dreamt it, well I know I was awake! You weren't there, you didn't see it right in front of your face, it didn't grab you, it grabbed me! Would a dream do this?" She raised her arm to show Matt where the clown had touched her. There was no denying that there was a clear, bright red mark in the shape of a hand print. Matt put his hand on it, it was still hot and it was starting to blister.

"Jesus, Jess, who did this to you?"

"THE CLOWN!" Jess screamed.

"Jess, I believe you, I believe you saw a clown, but what I'm saying is, it must have been someone dressed as a clown, someone who wanted to scare you, some sicko who maybe wanted to hurt you." Jess blinked at him, her face looked pained, almost as if she was pleading for a moment. She then violently shook her head.

"No. I know what I saw. I smelt it. No one else knew what I smelt when I was younger."

"What are you talking about? If it wasn't someone, Jess, who was it?" Matt exhaled a long and calculated breath. The pained expression returned to her face. She looked so lost. Although he hardly knew this woman, and although she seemed completely unstable and far too fragile to handle anything she was going through, he sensed a stubborn strength in her that he admired.

"I know what I saw," Jess repeated meekly. Matt walked over to her. He held her tightly until she stopped shaking.

"Ok Jess, I believe you," he lied. "Whatever it was though, broke into your house and tried to hurt you. So we still need to call the police. Ok?" She remained in his arms but silently nodded her head.

"I don't want to go back to the house alone though. Will you come with me?"

"Of course." Matt reluctantly let go of her and made his way to the telephone.

Chapter 8

Jess walked into the staffroom, keeping her eyes on each teacher as she passed them on her way to the kitchen area. As she stirred her coffee, any abnormal noise or particularly loud laugh would make her jump. Everything was the same. The room smelt of the cheap instant coffee they always supplied, the slightly stained furniture was still grey and unclean. The teachers all got on with one another but there were still cliques between the staff; looking around, that was also unchanged. The world around her was exactly the same as it was a week ago, but it no longer felt like it. Her world felt like it was upside down and it would never be the same again. She felt unsafe, afraid and alone. Even Matt and Dee did not believe her.

The police said they would talk to the circus, but she could tell that they did not believe her story either. In all fairness to them, it would be hard to ask a circus, especially one that advertised that they had no clowns, if they did in fact have clowns that ran around and terrorised people.

It was now believed between her friends that it was a break-in that had gone terribly wrong. When Jess reminded them that the police found no sign of a break-in and that the burglar had left without taking anything even after Jess had run out, their initial reply was to go silent for a second but then quickly dismiss it as Jess forgetting to lock the front door, allowing him to enter. The fact the thief had not taken anything could have just been because he had been equally as shaken after not expecting such an incident to happen.

She hated them. She hated everyone who could write everything off so rationally. They still thought she was justified in being scared and traumatised, although they just did not think she was correct as to why she was upset.

She hated every teacher who was sitting down and happily chatting away, living their lives so carefree. It was just not fair. She just didn't understand why any of this was happening, and what made her more terrified was that she was worried they may be right. What if she was wrong and was actually going crazy?

She hated them for making her doubt herself.

She spotted Dee had entered the room. The caring but blunt attitude her friend chose to give was not what she had needed recently, and nothing changed for Jess in the present. She tried to shrink and hide behind her cup but Dee knew where to look. Jess had stood and sipped her coffee in the same spot since they had known each other. Dee looked at Jess, gave a sympathetic smile and sat down. It wasn't the reaction Jess was expecting at all. Maybe Dee had finally come round to understanding what she was going through.

"Hi Jess, are you ok?" Whilst Jess was lost in her own thoughts, Louise, another teacher, had come over to her. They had always been friendly but in the three years they had worked together, had probably only said about 20 words to each other.

"Oh, hi Louise."

"I just heard about your break-in the other day and wanted to make sure you were okay." Her tone sounded rehearsed, nothing genuine about the performance she was acting out as she fluttered those unnaturally long lashes and played with her perfectly groomed blonde hair.

"Yes. I'm fine," Jess replied, slightly taken aback. "How do you know about that?"

"Oh it's a small town sweetheart. When someone dresses up as a clown whilst the circus is in town, breaks into your home and attacks you, well that isn't exactly an everyday thing is it?"

Jess clenched her jaw momentarily. "Well, I'm fine."

"Oh I just couldn't imagine what you went through," Louise continued. "You must be in such shock. If that ever happened to me, I wouldn't dream of going back into work so soon."

"Well I didn't like the idea of just sitting around in the house I was attacked in," Jess said dryly.

"Yes of course, dear. Well, either way, just checking up." Louise patted Jess's arm in such a patronising way that it made Jess actually feel violent towards everyone. Jess knew the break-in had been talked about, therefore, Jess knew she had also been talked about. Two days later and people were still interested in one of the strangest and scariest crimes that had happened in this town for a very long time.

"Do you think the clown is actually from the circus? Wouldn't it be an amazing way to cover your tracks? Pretend you don't have clowns, then use them to run all your criminal activity," one teacher had asked her, trying to get as much information out of her as possible.

"Maybe it's someone you know. Most crimes are committed by people you already know," was thoughtlessly asked by a parent of one of the school children whilst picking up their child the day before. This haunted Jess, and if she had to be honest with herself, was a theory she had not managed to shake off just yet.

It was not the questions that were bothering Jess so much, it was the insensitivity about how they were asked. They would ask all these questions, making Jess involuntarily relive the painful memories in her head, but they would never pay attention to the answer. They had already built up their own theories and stories and unless Jess simply confirmed them, no one really seemed to care anymore.

No one truly seemed concerned about Jess, and the people who did were handling it worse than anybody else.

"Jess I love you, but you can't go round telling people that a ghost clown attacked you. Those are the type of things that will have you placed in a padded cell for the rest of your life. You're a teacher, you can't seem so mentally unstable" was one of the many motivational speeches Dee had given to her in the last 48 hours. Which is why her sudden distance and shyness was peculiar, but also welcome.

Just as Jess was about to start feeling calm again, the head teacher, Mrs Hall, walked into the room. Jess sighed heavily as she knew she wasn't strong enough to go through another tedious staff meeting.

"Right, staff. Thank you so much for taking your time out while I go over some things," Mrs Hall began. "First off, I just want to remind you that parent's evening is closer than ever, so let's make sure we have everything ready. There is always going to be at least one parent who thinks they know better than us on how to educate a child. Remember, be honest, be firm, but above all, be professional when responding to the parents. Also, the circus trip will be tomorrow. Have all the students handed in their permission slips?" The teachers half-heartedly mumbled and nodded as Mrs Hall looked down at her notes. "Fantastic! No one likes to see a child left behind. Mr Healey, Miss Jones and erm... Miss Befria wasn't it? You will be the chaperones for tomorrow. Make sure you take your own lunch as the children will be taking theirs and that you are here for 8:30am. I know it's an early start for a Saturday, but I assure you, it will be a pleasant trip." Jess clenched down on her jaw so loudly there was an audible squeak of teeth. She stood there, silent and still as Mrs Hall finished her talk to a sleepy and disinterested staff room. When it was finally over, the teachers pulled themselves out of the chairs and started to make their way outside, moving silently and slowly, like a herd of zombies looking for their next meal. Jess walked straight to Mrs Hall, who was cleaning her notes away into an ugly, but smart satchel.

"Mrs Hall, could I speak to you?"

"Yes Miss Befria, what is it?"

"It's about tomorrow," Jess forced out.

"What about it?"

"I can't go."

"And why not?" Mrs Hall looked offended, like Jess had just turned down an invitation to the head teacher's very own wedding. Jess knew she could not tell the head teacher the truth, but she could at least play up to the rumours.

"The break-in. I was broken into. It was done by a man in a clown costume. I just don't feel safe going to the circus now."

"Oh yes." Mrs Hall nodded sympathetically. She pulled her eyebrows close together with a frown and Jess was amazed she could move her eyebrows at all with her bun tied back so tightly. "I heard about that, it truly was terrible and I am very sad to hear about it happen in such a nice area, but I'm afraid it's too short notice to cancel now. The school cannot permit only two chaperones. You don't want to disappoint all the other children, surely?"

Jess could not believe what she was hearing. How could she be so cold and business-like about the whole matter?

"You could make someone else go in my place."

"Look, Miss Befria, I am a very busy woman running a school, the staff and the children. There are no clowns in this circus, it was probably some teenage prank gone wrong. You will be fine and I'm not messing up school curriculums just because you don't feel up to it. All the other teachers have lives and have made plans with their own families now. Don't be so difficult and unprofessional." Jess had never been in a fight, but at this point, she had never felt so wounded in her life. She had worked so hard in everything she did, never complained, never spoke up, never did anything that could ever hurt or offend anyone, and the one time Jess needed help, no one believed her.

"Fine, Grace." Jess looked coldly into Mrs Hall's eyes with severity but keeping her face blank and hard to read.

"Mrs Hall, please."

"Fuck Mrs Hall." Only three words had left her mouth, but it was like dropping an atom bomb into the room. Everyone froze in their place, wide eyed and mouths agape. Staring in disbelief at what Jess had just said.

"How dare you speak to me like that!" Mrs Hall screeched.

"How dare you!" Jess knew that didn't have the same kick as swearing at her boss but she had snapped, she was one more sentence away from psychically lashing out on her, so she quickly turned around and stormed out of the teacher's lounge whilst everyone remained frozen on the spot and confused.

Jess sat in her pristine blue Ford Focus, both hands on the steering wheel, but she had no intention of starting the engine any time soon. She had stormed out of the teacher's lounge marching with no specific destination planned. She found herself in front of her car in the school carpark, got inside and sat down, and that was 30 minutes ago. Her hands were purely on the steering wheel to stop them from shaking so badly.

It was starting to go dark, winter was starting to set in with early nights and the air was turning suddenly crisp and cool. The harshness of the air was finally calming her down and the horror of what had happened was beginning to set in. She had verbally assaulted her boss. She can still remember how wide-eyed Mrs Hall had looked, how thin her lips went as every muscle in Mrs Hall's body noticeably clenched. There was no way around it, Jess was going to get fired. Gross misconduct, with every teacher present to witness it. Although, she did wonder why no one had come to find her and why Mrs Hall had not come out by now to find her. Maybe they just assumed she had left by now. Maybe they assumed Jess had quit and she would not even have to go the circus tomorrow. Because of this they would find someone late notice - the only saving grace to this whole mess. Jess could not afford to lose her job and could not believe that she had allowed anything in her life to take over in such a way that she could lose control like that. She looked down at her petite hands, slightly chipped blue nail varnish that matched the neat and ironed blue shirt she was wearing, wondering when the next time would be needed for her to wear a shirt. She flopped her head against the steering wheel, allowing her flat, brown hair to fall around her face. She was trying to convince herself this was for the best, that she never really wanted to work there in the first place, when suddenly she heard a knock on the car window. Startled, she looked to the passenger seat, and there was Matt leaning over to look through the window. Jess sighed, leaned over and unlocked the car door. Matt got into the car, closed the door, rubbing his hands together for warmth, but kept his eyes forward the whole time, never looking at her.

"It's getting cold all of a sudden," Matt said. Jess hung her head, staring at her knees. "Getting dark too," he continued.

"What do you want Matt?"

"Isn't it obvious?" He turned his head and stared at Jess. She looked at him and their eyes locked onto each other, his dark brown eyes seemed to pierce into her soul and she could feel her cheeks begin to burn.

"Is it?" she asked.

"The warmth." He smiled, then started to blow into his hands. Jess turned away hoping he didn't notice just how red she had turned.

"Am I fired?" Jess braced herself.

"No."

"No?"

"No," Matt repeated. Jess didn't really know how to respond to this. She wanted to act relieved, but her pride and embarrassment would not allow her to do that.

"I find that hard to believe." This seemed to be the only response that made sense for her to say.

"I'm not going to lie Jess, Grace was pretty set on letting you go initially. You swore at her. She wants to give people a disciplinary who call her by the first name, and I think that includes the parents." Matt tried to joke.

"So what made her change her mind?"

Matt ran his fingers through his messy hair. So much had fallen out of the pony tail now, it was barely worth having the hair tie in. You could tell that he had been playing with his hair an extra amount today, nerves maybe.

"Because I talked to her," he admitted.

"You did? Saying what?"

"I just reminded her that you have just been through something that was a genuine traumatising experience. That it was unprofessional of her to act so cold, which really wound her up by the way. You're an amazing teacher and Dee had a word or two to say as well. We wouldn't have let you get fired."

Jess felt her eyes begin to sting from the tears she was fighting back. She could not stand that she had become such a mess that she needed her friends to look after her and fight her battles, but still, she was overwhelmed with gratitude. It also explained why Mrs Hall had not come out looking for her. She leaned into Matt and placed her hand over his and squeezed.

"Matt, thank you. You didn't have to do that." Matt smiled, looked at her so intently and then lowered his gaze.

"There is, however, one problem."

"What is it?" Her heart started to pound at what this problem could be.

"You have to go to the circus tomorrow."

"I thought I had no choice in the matter anyway?" Jess scoffed with venom.

"Me and Dee tried to get you replaced, to the point even other teachers finally volunteered to go instead of you, but I guess Grace is being a sadistic bitch over this now. She insists it must be you because if not, then you will win or something, I don't know. Basically she's saying, if you go to the circus, she will drop everything, if not, you'll probably get a written disciplinary."

"But what I did was gross misconduct, I'll be fired on the spot."

"Or you go to the circus."

"Matt, you know I can't."

"Honestly, Jess, I think you should."

"Why? So I don't lose my job?" Jess spat out.

"No, for so much more now. I truly see how much pain you are in for you to react like that to someone. You didn't even complain if someone gave you the completely wrong meal in a restaurant for Christ sake. I honestly think that going to the circus will be good for you, for you to see that whatever horrible things have happened to you, happened in the past and it's over."

"So you don't believe me either then?"

"I never said that."

"If you believed me, you would accept that going back is not an option."

"Jess, I truly believe whatever happened to you, happened. I just don't think your demons are in that place anymore. You need to fight this, and me and Dee will be there." Matt grabbed Jess's free hand and squeezed it tightly, then pulled her closer to him. "We will be there for you and I will be holding your hand the entire way." They were now so close their noses were grazing each other's. His warm but sweet breath was washing over Jess's face and she felt intoxicated.

"Promise?" Jess whispered.

"Jess, I'll never let you go for a second." Jess completely forgot about the circus, Mrs Hall or even Dee for a moment and finally allowed herself to want Matt. They sat in silence staring at each other, both wanting to kiss but both too afraid so soon. Eventually Matt raised up Jess's hand and kissed the back of it.

"Jess, you can do anything. Let's go to the circus." Jess never understood if it was just the sudden release of oxytocin from thinking about kissing him that made her feel so brave or just sheer stupidity, but either way, she was smiling.

"Yeah, let's go to the circus."

Chapter 9

Lying in her bed, she stared at the ceiling. The clock read 6:30am and she knew she needed to get up and get ready soon. Her momentary bravery from the day before had long vanished and she had resumed back to absolute fear mixed in with embarrassment every time she remembered her public outburst with the head teacher.

Jess was finally returning to the same circus she had visited 20 years previously. Twenty years after that horrific ordeal that had always plagued her and constantly turned her dreams into nightmares.

Everyone thought she was overreacting, but if someone who suffers from arachnophobia was asked to bathe in a bathtub full of tarantulas and they outright refused to, people would understand that; because it's a common fear among people. No one understood Jess or her problem. She was alone.

Jess's fingers seem to glide over every item of clothing she had as she picked out her outfit. She never usually cared so much, but everything about today had a sense of urgency to it. Even the attire had to be meticulously planned. Nothing could be forgotten about. Flats not heels, in case she had to run. Trousers not a skirt, in case she had to climb. Long sleeved shirt, not short sleeved, in case the clown grabbed her again.

She packed light, she did not want anything to weigh her down, she drank coffee to wake herself up and be alert and, after checking every room before locking it all up, she left the house. It saddened her she had to be so thorough with every room before leaving and entering the house. This new habit of hers had only formed after the break-in.

She steadily drove to the school, repeating over and over in her head that she would be ok. The clouds were heavy and dark in the sky, it looked like there could be a thunderstorm at any moment. She arrived at the school and stared at her place of work - she did not want to enter it. She told herself that she felt unsafe everywhere, including her home, so it should not really make a difference where she went. She walked around the building to the main entrance, where she could already hear the excited children scream and giggle. As she approached the entrance she could see she was the final chaperone to arrive. Mrs Hall was standing there too with a clipboard and Jess's heart stopped momentarily. Mrs Hall gave Jess a sharp look, her lips, thin and closed tight, her eyes became so squinted that she almost looked like they were closed. It was obvious she had not forgotten the previous evening.

"Miss Befria," she addressed sternly.

"Mrs Hall," Jess squeaked back. Mrs Hall's lips softened slightly and her eyes opened a little to take in Jess more. The correct way of addressing each other had noticeably relaxed her. This allowed Jess to loosen up slightly too. All she had to do was go on this school trip and she might actually get away with calling her boss by the unthinkable; her first name. Mrs Hall finally took her gaze away from Jess and returned her attention to the children, rounding them up and making them pick a friend to be their partner for the rest of the day. Lining them up in twos, checking they all had their lunch, whilst fighting to be heard against a group of energetic children.

Jess did not move, she was too scared to draw any more attention to herself than she already had. Instead, she just stood there watching Mrs Hall arrange everything, then looked over to the other side of the children where Dee and Matt were standing. They were already watching Jess. Dee was watching her with that sympathetic doe-eyed look which unnerved Jess more than anything else. Matt was looking at her with a warm expression. He gave her a playful smirk and it made her stomach do somersaults, and her mind quickly raced back the evening before in the carpark. Not a word had been spoken between the three chaperones just yet as the school bus pulled up in front of everyone.

"Right children! Get in twos with your partner, *calmly* get on the bus and take a seat. Let's do this quickly and efficiently. Also, remember, the circus is being very nice and letting us go in before official opening times for this trip, so be on your best behaviour. You are representing the school. If you misbehave, we will know about it."

The children scrambled onto the bus, fought over seats and one child tripped over what she claimed was John Michael's foot, who mischievously swore he had done absolutely nothing. The three chaperones stood outside the bus whilst Mrs Hall tried to calm them down one more time before exiting the vehicle. Mrs Hall climbed down the steps and looked the three of them up and down.

"School trips are never the easiest. Please be professional whilst representing the school, we don't want to lose a child or worse because you are not 100% alert." She finished this sentence whilst staring directly at Jess. Jess felt a sudden urge to lash out again but she was determined to be better than that this time.

"Yes, Mrs Hall," the three said in unison, which made them all crack a slight smile whilst trying to suppress a giggle. For a moment they felt like three school children themselves, getting told off. Mrs Hall's face remained flat and expressionless, she walked back to the school with her clipboard without saying a single word. The three stood in an almost awkward silence, Jess not really sure if she was going to get on this bus and her two friends not sure how to be around Jess today either.

"Well. I guess we better get going," Jess exclaimed, trying as hard as she could to sound normal.

"Are you sure?" Dee asked, putting a hand on her arm, making Jess question if Dee had been taken over by some pod person. Dee had always been protective and caring of Jess, but Dee was going into overdrive recently. She had rung up to check on Jess every other hour the night before, making sure she was ok. Jess felt like her best friend was unintentionally killing her with kindness.

"Yes, I'm an adult, I need to act like one. I'm fine, let's not keep these kids waiting any longer or else they might rip a chair out or something." Forcing out a giggle, Jess started to enter the double decker bus.

"I'll go upstairs and keep an eye on the kids there," Jess volunteered.

"I'll go with you," Matt said.

"Oh sure, leave me down here to struggle alone," Dee retorted.

"You know all the well behaved kids are sat down here. You could even sleep on the way there and nothing would happen," Jess smugly informed Dee.

"Yeah, yeah, just don't let me find you two kissing on the back seat if I come up," Dee teased, smiling as she went to sit down next to a little girl begging for her favourite teacher to sit next to her.

Jess quickly climbed up the little spiral steps to get to the upper floor so no one could see just how much she was blushing from that remark. She had no idea if Dee actually knew just how close her and Matt came to kissing the night before or if it was just a harmless joke, but either way, Jess was not a good liar. She felt guilty for wanting Matt, knowing Dee liked him too. However, Dee's attention on Matt had relaxed very quickly over the last week, so Jess could not help hoping Dee was not interested anymore.

Her appearance was clearly not welcome by a small group of boys who grumbled whilst very quickly stuffing something back into their pockets as Jess reached the top deck of the bus. She pretended not to have seen them and went to the front row of worn down seats and sat down. Very soon after, Matt followed her and sat beside her. The engine spluttered and roared to life, moving with a rather violent jolt and almost knocking some people out of their seats, but that did not upset the children, they just got more excited and started to cheer and clap as they were now officially on their way.

"I'm so proud of you, Jess," Matt whispered under his breath, covered by all the screaming.

"What, that I didn't punch Grace in the mouth before?" Jess joked.

"For everything. You will see just how good this is for you when you get there."

"I hope so, Matt, I really do."

The closer they were to the circus, the weaker Jess felt. Her hands were starting to clam up and her chest started to get tight. She could not understand how she had allowed herself to get into this situation. As they were driving along the road she started to see flyers and posters stuck on lamp posts and walls saying that it was close by. Her stomach turned at the sight of the posters. By the time the bus had turned into the actual venue and started to park up, Jess felt so weak that she could collapse right there in the chair and was even more grateful she had decided on wearing flat shoes. She did not want to seem unstable in front of the children but she also doubted that she would be able to stand without throwing up. She looked at Matt, who actually seemed concerned when he looked at her.

"Do I look that bad?" she asked herself, knowing that she probably did.

"I'll lead the kids out first, you follow us. You sure you're ok?" he asked patiently.

"Yes... I'm fine," she lied.

Matt stood and started to bark orders at all the children whilst still managing to keep a friendly but authoritative tone. He got them to line up as calmly as he could manage and then led the way off the bus.

Jess was still sitting in the chair when she realised all the children were off. She looked out of the back window and at the edge of the carpark she could see the bright colours of tents.

"I can't do this," she realised. She was holding on to the seat with both hands, shaking and out of breath. She was about to cry when she heard footsteps coming back up the stairs. She looked in the direction of the stairs to see Matt, coming back for her.

"Jess."

"Don't. Don't tell me I can, because I can't, I thought I could but I was wrong and I don't care if I get fired, I'm not going and no one can make me." Matt walked over to her, got onto his knees and held her hand. She broke away from her destructive thoughts for a moment and allowed herself to look at him. His eyes pierced into hers and she could tell he meant every word he said to her.

"Jess, no one is going to make you do anything. We all care for you and will be here for you. If you don't want to, then don't. But I honestly think this is the best thing you could ever do. You're facing your fears. It's how people get over shit that's happened to them Jess, and you do can do it. I *know* you can."

"You don't know anything. You barely know me. I've known you a week, no one is this nice to someone after only a week."

"I know enough." He leaned in close again, their noses almost brushing, and she could feel his warm breath brush her face as he breathed. For a moment she forgot where she was and felt fearless towards everything and everyone. "Show the kids how much of a badass you are," he instructed.

"Ok, you *really* don't know me," she scoffed, smiling and wiping away a solitary tear. She fell silent for a moment before continuing to talk. "Do you think I'm crazy?"

"What? No! I just think you're dealing with a lot of crap that you've never really dealt with."

"I think Dee thinks I'm crazy, she's stopped preaching and now just smiles at me like she's worried I'm about to go on a murder spree or something," she rambled on whilst Matt laughed.

"Jess, she's being nice because I made her be nice. I told her to ease up on you, I made her realise that tough love isn't the right kind of love that works on everyone."

"You silenced Dee? My Dee? My best friend, the most opinionated person in the world, Dee? You're not a teacher, you're a magician." Jess smiled, stood up and held Matt's hand. Another pregnant pause took place as they stared at each other for a little too long.

"Thank you," she said quietly. "I honestly don't think I would be here right now if it wasn't for you." She let go of his hand and calmly walked down the stairs. The children did not seem to notice her absence but Dee was staring at her, searching for any signs of distress. Jess nodded to her whilst giving an "*I'm fine*" look that seemed to satisfy Dee for now. The weather was still dry but the carpark was just a field that they had pitched their circus and everything on, so the mud was loose and damp from the cars and feet constantly going over it. The circus had a temporary white picket fence placed around the perimeter of the circus and dividing the carpark too. They had placed a wide open gate in it for people to leave the carpark and enter the circus area. No one was around, it was quiet and only a couple of cars were dotted about. There were a couple of little stalls and booths. A box office trailer was right at the front to remind everyone this was not a free event. There were two outside trailer toilets to use, and at the back of the plot was the huge big top with its iconic red and white stripes running down from the very top. The children were getting restless. They wanted to run inside but they had been allowed to come in early before the first show so nowhere was open just yet and they had to remain patient until further instructions.

Dee went over to the ticket office at the front to talk to someone. Jess could not stop feeling on edge, watched even. She constantly kept shifting her eyes to the left and then to the right. Always on guard for anything that could happen. She kept mentally counting in her head to ten and then would count backwards to zero to try and distract her anxiety and calm herself.

Dee returned with a couple of flyers and a strip of tickets the length of her entire body, like the ones you would win on machines in arcades.

"Ok children, listen up," Dee commanded. "The circus opens at 10am for everybody and the first show is at 11. It's now 9:15 and we are very lucky because we have been allowed in early before anybody else so we can have a look around the big top, get a tour of the trailers and even look at the animals back stage!" The children started to squeal and giggle with excitement but Jess could feel her knees about to go so she counted faster to herself.

"So first things first children, let's get in a line of two with our partners and wait until the Ringmaster gets here, ok?" Dee finished. The children clamoured around, eager to get on with the day; eventually they all found a place in line next to their partners and stood there eagerly looking around for someone to show up. Soon they saw a tall, grey haired man walk up to them. He had a thick build with a round stomach and a perfectly groomed moustache. He was carrying a tall and shiny black top hat under his arm whilst wearing black, high horse riding boots, with white pants tucked into them that matched the neatly ironed shirt tucked into the trousers. His bright red waistcoat was immaculate. Jess could not help but be impressed at how much he could keep a garment so clean around all the mud and animals.

"Good morning children!" his voice boomed, the children fell silent, instantly in awe. "I am Billy Bob and this is my circus! This circus started in 1915 when my grandfather brought his growing circus over from America. Our family have a great amount of respect for tradition so we've never let it leave our family! We have a little museum in the back which we will allow you to see a little later on, but first, who wants to see some animals?"

The children roared in excitement and the Ringmaster laughed.

"Well then, follow me!" He put on the hat he was carrying and started to walk towards the big top. As they walked into the tent, there was a little entrance foyer. There was a hot dog and candy floss stall, a photo booth and a handful of picnic tables. There were two openings beside the entrance, Billy Bob pointed at the smaller one explaining that the door was the entrance to the museum they would later see and that the larger entrance was to the actual big top ring where the shows were performed. He walked through the big entrance and pushed some heavy red velvet curtains aside, revealing the huge ring with seats circling half of it, the other half had openings for the backstage area. It was much darker in here, the only lights were artificial and as there was no actual show being performed at the moment, only a minimal amount of lights were left on.

Jess's eyes darted around the room. There were support pillars to keep the tent up that loomed overhead with ropes and bridges attached for parts of the show. Every empty seat seemed to cast an unnaturally long shadow onto the one behind it and eventually create tall eerie shadows onto the back of the tent due to the only lights that were on being close to the floor. It unsettled Jess; she kept expecting every shadow to move, she kept counting over and over but she could also feel a bead of sweat start to trickle down her forehead.

The Ringmaster then led them around the ring until they made it to the very back. He lifted up the tent curtains and allowed everyone to pass through first before he followed. The floor was grass, just like around the entire circus, but backstage was also littered with sawdust. This room was almost as big as the main stage, filled with props neatly placed and stored around the doors for easy access during the show. On the other side were some animals fenced in their own little wooden or caged pens so they could not run away.

"Billy Bob's Circus used to have over 20 types of animals, from dogs to elephants. However, as the years have gone on, we have to think of the animals' health above entertainment, it's no longer practical or safe to be taking elephants from town to town so now we keep it small, we have a pet dog, two horses, five doves, two rabbits and even a snake!" The children looked around eagerly for the snake, some through excitement, others through trepidation.

"Don't worry," the Ringmaster comforted, "the snake is asleep in his home right now."

For the rest of the tour the Ringmaster would take the children one by one around the room to see each animal. He would tell them their names and what job they had to do in each performance. Whiskers the dog did his own little act; chasing a ball his master would pretend to throw off stage, he would then come back with a giant ball, confusing his master and making the crowd laugh. The two horses, Jekyll and Hyde, were part of a gymnastic act where a petite lady would hop between both horses whilst they would run around the perimeter of the ring, eventually ending up doing a handstand with one hand on each horse. This was an incredibly difficult and dangerous trick which Billy Bob stressed should not be tried at home. The doves and rabbits were part of a magic act which he would explain no further as "*a magician never reveals their tricks.*" The snake was called Stretch and was part of a belly dancing routine where the lady would reveal the inside of a giant wicker basket, which would be empty. She then began to dance as a rope would start to rise from inside the open basket. She would then start to climb the rising rope. When the music stopped the rope would go limp and the rope and herself would fall into the basket. As impressive as all that sounded, her grand finale would be to then come back out with the long snake wrapped around her.

The children were in awe; hearing parts of the show had not ruined any of the surprise but merely increased their excitement and made them even more impatient.

Jess could not believe this was the same circus she had attended when she was seven years old. She remembered the acts, the animals and her own excitement to be here. It had all changed. She did not recognise anything except the tent itself. She was starting to calm down slightly - this was not the circus that had scarred her past. Every minute she spent in the tent made her realise she must have been making the whole thing up. Just how much she had completely built something up in her head was terrifying alone. Maybe everyone was right, maybe someone tried to scare her when she was young and she has just been forcing all the pieces to fit lately. She was so ashamed, embarrassed, she was a teacher who had to look after these children and she had almost refused to get off the bus this morning.

The rest of the day went by very quickly. They had been shown around the trailers where the performers would live in whilst on the road. They even bumped into one or two of them and they said hello whilst the children stared at them like celebrities. The performance was flawless, it was even better than Billy Bob had described and the children loved every second of it. During the performance, if the lights went out suddenly for dramatic effect or if there was a particularly loud noise, Jess would start to jump about and fidget nervously. Going to the circus had cured a lot of her anxiety but she had not completely recovered just yet.

After the show they had some lunch on the picnic tables whilst Jess actually had to admit to herself she felt ok, calm even at times. Although, she was not looking forward to the responses and expressions she would receive off Matt and Dee when she finally admitted this to them.

Once the lunches were eaten and everything was packed away, the Ringmaster returned for the final part of their tour.

"Well children, did you enjoy the show?" he asked, and the children half roared their response or rapidly spoke over each other, telling Billy Bob what their favourite part of the show was. He raised his hands to signal he needed silence and they complied.

"Well, I'm really glad you enjoyed my little circus, and I do hope if we ever find our way back here, you will make sure you tell all your family and friends about us! Now though boys and girls, it's time for the final part of the tour. You've seen what the circus is like today, but let's take you back in time with our little museum, showing you what the circus used to be like through the decades! Follow me." The children obediently followed; he had such a strong but kind voice, you instantly liked him, he was calming with a protective nature.

Inside the tent, what they called their museum, was very small. It was low lit and draped once again with many heavy velvet curtains. They clearly showed a lot of pride towards the history of the circus but Jess noticed none of them mentioned the murderous clown. She looked at old props on little stands with plaques explaining the use this item once had, but what she could not help admire most were the old photographs framed and hanging by string from above or nailed to perfectly black painted boards. They dated back decades; some were newspaper clippings that had been framed, showing just how popular this circus had been back in its prime. Jess stared intently at every photograph whilst the children restrained themselves with difficulty not to touch anything.

Jess eventually came up to a photograph, worn but coloured, of a bunch of people standing outside the circus, labelled 'Staff 1976.' She stared at every face wondering if they were still here, or even still alive. She came to the end of the first row in the photograph and nearly screamed. Right there, plainly dressed in the photograph, was the man she dreamt of in that caravan hurting that boy and girl. The photograph was faded but there was no mistaking it, that was the man that haunted her. That was the man with demon black eyes, the clown who was terrorising her and the murderer who killed children, not just in her dreams, but in real life. She had not made this up, she had not imagined anything, how could she have known?

"Ah, you're admiring me in my youth." The Ringmaster spoke gently and proudly behind her. Jess jumped, not realising she was being watched.

"I'm sorry?" Jess squeaked.

"Ah, yes, I suppose I look a little different now," he chuckled, whilst patting his much wider stomach now. "But that strapping young man was me in my prime." He placed his finger on the man in her nightmares. "Back then I was just cleaning out the horses. You have to earn your keep in the circus and work your way up, even if your father did run the circus."

"That's not the clown?" asked Jess. Billy Bob scrunched his face, confused as to why she would ask this but too polite to question it.

"Well, no, that was the clown." Billy Bob pointed to a gaunt, sad face that appeared in his mid 30's standing two rows behind. "When we had clowns, that is. I suppose you've heard the rumours. No matter how far we try to run, they always follow."

"I heard something, didn't think too much of it," Jess lied.

"Yes, it was sad what happened to those children. He was the last clown we ever had. Such a shame," he repeated solemnly.

"What was his name?" Jess asked.

"David Benson. Quiet man, stuttered a lot, so he didn't like to talk much."

"No, I meant, what was his clown name? Stage name I mean?" Even Jess did not understand why she asked this question. The Ringmaster stared at the photograph for a long time with a solemn expression. He turned at Jess, and she stared straight into his eyes, which were darker than she realised this morning, and answered with only one word before walking away.

"Peekaboo."

Chapter 10

"Jess, what is going on, why won't you talk to me?"

"Matt, I'm fine, I just have something I need to do."

"What is it though? Tell me, I can help."

"You can't... not with this. I'm sorry. I'll call you later I promise."

"You said that yesterday, but you didn't. And the night before. I'm worried"

"I'm sorry, I will tonight, I promise."

Jess hated lying to Matt but it was the only way to get him off the phone. She felt she was mistaken in trusting him with her fears in the past; people all looked at her as if she was crazy. If she had told Matt that she may have dreamt events that actually happened in the past, they would lock her up in a padded room and throw away the key. This time Jess would be smarter than that - everything she suspected and found out, she would do alone and keep to herself.

She looked around her living room. Every room in her house had always been immaculate, with white or pastel colours and minimal decoration. Her living room now had the appearance of what the aftermath of a paper storm would look like. Sheets of paper carpeted the floor, whilst various clippings were strewn over the coffee table. On one wall Jess had pinned, taped and even glued directly onto her walls; pictures, printed articles and anything else she could come across to do with the history of Billy Bob's Circus and the case of the murdered children.

The history of the circus was pretty straight forward. It started small in America, brought over to the UK in 1915, just like Billy Bob had told them, and not much more was to be said about the circus until 1979. Two children were reported missing after going to the circus with their friends. They both broke away from the group and were never seen alive again. The friends of the missing children had reported to the police that they saw their friends talking to a clown at the circus, away from the group. The police went back to the circus to investigate. The clown, by the name of David Benson, had been a law-abiding man up to this point and suffered from a terrible stammer. The published police report had said he was quiet, friendly and helpful. However, when allowed to search his living space, they found the two children, a girl and a boy, unnaturally stuffed into a large suitcase. David admitted to the crime, crying on the bed; the report had put that he refused to go without a fight. He doused himself with lighter fuel from his nightstand and lit a match, trying to kill himself and the police officers too. The officers managed to escape thankfully with the bodies of the children, but David Benson and all the other evidence was burnt to ashes that night. After that, the Billy Bob Circus had become famous overnight for all the wrong reasons. No one wanted to go. They were too afraid of the new reputation that now followed the circus around, so in 1981 it was made official that there would never be another clown to work for that circus again.

When it came to hard facts, this is where the story ended. Nothing else happened, no more murders were tied to David Benson or the circus in general, people started to become morbidly intrigued about the murder stories as the years passed, and soon enough, they were a normal circus again, but without clowns.

What had sent Jess into a research frenzy, causing her home to be wrapped in paper, was what she kept finding after those dates. On numerous forums across the internet there were countless people claiming to have seen a clown at this circus. There were even three police reports stating that a man dressed as a clown had tried to abduct children. One police report was in Chester in 1987, another in Salford in 1990 and the third in York in 2002. All the stories were surprisingly similar online as well. Everyone who had encountered the clown was a child at the time, no more than ten. No one else claimed to have seen the clown but them, and the final similarity that sent a chill down Jess's spine just thinking about it was the fact that every encounter described the man as on fire, burnt or glowing. Naturally none of these police reports went any further; all were believed to be hoaxes or pranks played on the victims, but Jess knew all too well what was true and what was not.

She had printed off every story, report and even found a drawing someone had sketched from memory. She even tried to find out who these mysterious victims were and if she could contact them at all, but she was currently hitting nothing but dead ends. She had struck gold however, when stumbling across a supernatural forum, a link to a blog written by a man who had claimed to be suffering from the ghost revisiting him now he was an adult. Jess could not believe she was not alone in this. She had eagerly clicked on the link, hungry for information so she could connect more dots together. There was only one entry in his blog.

June 21st 2010

I'm writing this because I feel I have to put a message out to someone who will listen. I can only hope at least one of you will believe me. My name is Peter Neil. I am a 37 year old man. I am a father. I am a husband. I am a scientist. I also worry I may be crazy.

When I was 9 years old I went to a circus, Billy Bob's Spectacular Circus to be precise, and a clown attacked me. I do not remember much, but I was young, he was on fire and I was scared. The Circus argued with my parents, I remember that. They thought I was causing trouble because only the year before they had officially announced that they would no longer have clowns at all in the show. My parents believed the Ringmaster and grounded me for a week. I was so angry, hurt and alone that no one believed me. They thought I was simply a child with an overactive imagination so I dedicated my life to being able to explain things. I worked hard at school, studied physics in university, followed by a master's and then on to a PHD and I now lecture at the University of Exeter. However, I do hope you know that I am not here to boast about my education. I am merely trying to point out to you, that I am in fact an educated man. I have dedicated my life to a profession of solving the unsolved, and we do this through hypothesis and experiments. I constantly have to keep a level head, think of all possibilities and disprove something to prove another.

It is important to me that you understand I am a sane and stable person because what I am about to write will make you doubt that, but I will not blame you, because experiencing it made me doubt my sanity myself. After all this though, I know who I am. I know I am sane and I know this is real.

Two weeks ago we started to see flyers for a circus. It was Billy Bob's Spectacular Circus and I recognised it straight away as the same one I went to as a child. Their logo and colours had barely changed. The moment my 5 year old son and 7 year old daughter saw this, they pleaded with me to take them. I am not a man who lets traumatising events in my past debilitate me; on the contrary, I embrace them. Especially this one, going to the circus and no one believing had impregnated me with a seed that never stopped growing. A thirst I could never quench for answers to anything I didn't understand. I always laugh at the vicious circle however, as I always felt the more you learn, the less you know.

I decided I would take the children on the weekend as my beautiful wife was not working then either and we could go as the happy family we are, 99% of the time. Or should I say, were.

There was not much to say about that first day, when the circus was in town, if you had asked me then, I would not have thought anything of it. Looking back now I remembered that I was always hot, it was June so I thought it was just the weather but it was not a particularly hot day and I was always sweating. I also kept smelling something that was burning, something horrible. That night was the first night I had the dream. I was outside a circus, time would move unusually in this dream and it was so lucid and so vivid I could feel the cold air on my skin or smell the food from the vending trailers. I always seemed to know where to go with no direction needed, not into the big top where the show was, but behind it, where the accommodation trailers were. I never tried to open any of the doors, but through the windows, as if watching a film play out, I watched horrific scenes of murder, torture and fire.

After I dreamt the dream for the first time, I woke up in a pool of sweat. Terrified. My wife calmed me down, reminding me it was only a dream, and on that particular occasion it worked and I went back to sleep. The dream, however, was persistent. It returned every night, showing me more and more until I was afraid to sleep. By the fourth night I was determined to stay up all night whilst I researched the cognitive causes for night terrors. I had a theory that this was repressed anxiety from my childhood, manifesting into something much worse. There was a boy and girl in my dream, they were not my children, but maybe they were meant to represent them, maybe I felt I was not being a good father, maybe I was failing them. Maybe I was just more afraid of clowns and some stupid circus than I had let myself believe. Around 2:00am I noticed I could smell the same burning smell I noticed a couple of days prior. I hunted through the house looking for it but found nothing. When I entered my study again and closed the door, someone was waiting for me; behind the door was the clown I saw when I was 9. He was still dressed in his dirty clothes and his wounds across half of his body and face were glowing, as if the fire had just gone out but the embers would still burn if you touched them. He said nothing. He stared at me for a moment and then attacked me, his touch burning a mark on my arm I can still see now, a week later. I somehow managed to get away, I grabbed the kids and woke the wife and we stayed at my parents' house that night whilst I called the police. They found no signs of breaking and entering. They said they would investigate the circus but also reminded us that the circus did not have clowns. I felt history repeating itself.

Over the next 6 days I would be visited by this clown every night. The dreams have also gotten worse. My work has suffered, I never sleep. My wife is currently not talking to me and has taken the children to stay at her own mother's as she thinks I am insane and does not want the children around me. What broke my heart was as the children were taken away my little boy whispered "I believe you, I see him too," and then got in the car. I know I will see them again, I just need to prove what I am seeing.

After almost two weeks I began to believe that the clown was not terrorising me but possibly trying to communicate with me. The clown had taken steps to write things. It is minimal but I believed he was trying to leave clues. He only ever wrote the word 'Peekaboo'. Once in my steamed up bathroom mirror whilst I was washing and the other he spelt out with the magnetic letters we had on our fridge door. I later learnt it was his stage name when he performed in the circus himself. Billy Bob's circus.

I have noticed whenever he is in the room, I can smell burning, but sometimes I can feel drastic temperature changes and this is what I find the most interesting. Usually people claim to have seen a ghost and will say that the room goes cold. Scientists suggest, if they believe in ghosts that is, that cold spots occur because one of the main theories is that ghosts are energy and in order to manifest, they have to pull energy, that is heat, from the environment. The temperature only changes when I see this clown and he is more than glowing, he is actually on fire or if he has written something. The temperature rise also varies. I can go from one room that is cold to the next room being significantly warmer and that is it, or I could find myself in a room that instantly gets so hot I start to sweat. I wonder if he is always trying to break through whatever glass wall is stopping him from interacting with us completely. Maybe he is stronger around people who can see him.

I will not lie, I am afraid. I have now researched a lot about the circus and I have read what this clown is meant to be. A murderer. I am at a loss though, because I feel my dreams could be telling me something else and this is what the clown is trying to say to me.

Please remember, I am an educated, scientific man. I know a ghost clown sending me messages in my sleep sounds insane. I am exhausted and not myself from the sleep deprivation and this post is merely a desperate attempt to reach out to someone who has been through the same thing.

The circus is leaving tomorrow night and I need answers. I am going to go speak to them.

Wish me luck,
Peter Neil.

Every word written had given Jess a morbid hope. She hated reading the words on her screen - knowing that others had gone through this somehow made it even more real. It also gave her hope, however, that there was at least someone out there who believed her and may even know how to fix everything. She saw a couple of people reply to the post wishing him luck, confirming they had seen the ghost when they were a kid but never when they were adults, or some people just completely mocked him and his story. She did wonder why he had never replied after five years with an update. She searched his name online and found her answer. Two days after that post was published, on June 23rd, Peter Neil was officially reported missing by his wife, who had become more and more concerned when he had not answered the phone for two days. His body was never found.

Jess simply sat there in silence for an hour after discovering this. She had come so close to an answer for it then to be ripped away from her so quickly. She wondered if he was murdered, had ran away or maybe he even killed himself. She would never know, and neither would his wife, and Jess's heart hurt for her. No family should go through that.

Jess was printing off the fifth story she had found on paranormal-encounters.com when she heard a knock at the door. The noise startled her and made her jump. She was not expecting anyone so she moved slowly to the front door, unable to see who it was through the solid oak.

"Who's there?" she called out, before opening the door.

"It's me, Matt." Jess sighed with relief, although she wasn't quite sure who she was expecting it to be. She opened the door to Matt, standing there with a bottle of wine.

"What do you want Matt?" she asked with a tired but warm tone.

"I just thought you may want to fill me in on why you haven't been in work for a week. Plus, it's a Friday and I think you could do with the company." Jess looked over her shoulders uneasily, staring at the chaotic paper trail in her living room.

"That's really sweet Matt, but I'm busy. I'll be back in work on Monday, I'm fine, just been a little under the weather that's all."

"Oh really? Because there is a little rumour going around that you never take a sick day. So for you to be off for five days must be much worse than just a little under the weather."

"I must have caught something on the school trip, must be worse than I realised." Jess put a hand to her head and tried to pull an expression of pain.

"Jess, you are a terrible liar. We are all worried about you, let me inside."

"But if I do, you will be more worried," Jess blurted out. Matt's face was more confused than ever but she could see the genuine concern in his face, and she felt such a pang of guilt for pushing him away and lying to him for almost a week. It had not felt like a week that she had avoided anyone and fixated on her research, but it was something she needed to do right now and did not expect anyone to understand. She looked down at her mismatched PJ's she was wearing. She could not even remember when she had changed, washed or even brushed her hair. At the very least, she must look the part of a terribly sick person. However, standing in front of Matt, tall, clean and groomed, she felt a flush of embarrassment.

"I look a mess," she stated apologetically.

"Yes you do," Matt laughed, looking at her, "but still pretty. Now let me in." Jess seriously considered letting him. Telling him everything and completely trusting him to believe her and support her, but she could not. She could not risk having one more judgemental or sympathetic look thrown her way. No, this she had to do alone. She harnessed every fibre of her lacking acting skills.

"Matt, seriously, I'm just ill, I don't want you to get it too. Can I call you tomorrow?" Matt stared at her, clearly unsure how to act, but eventually something must have won in the internal fight he seemed to be having because his shoulders slumped slightly and he sighed heavily.

"Are you sure you're ok?" he persisted.

"Better than ever, and I truly do appreciate you checking up on me. I'll call you tomorrow ok?" Matt leaned in to kiss her on the cheek but she noticed he was trying to stare over her shoulder and try to see into her house. If he had seen the mess she had made, his expression did not show it. He smiled at her and walked away, defeated. She watched him walk halfway down the path and then closed the door.

She walked back into the living room, hungry to continue her research, but when she walked into the room she noticed straight away, scrawled over eight pieces of A4 paper stuck to the wall, big red letters spelling out the word *Peekaboo*. Jess felt her veins go cold and hard, like her blood was now ice. She became unable to move from the fear of how those letters got there and who wrote them. She suddenly regretted not letting Matt in; crazy or not, she would be safer with someone in the house with her. That was when she noticed the smell. Burning hair entered her nostrils and turned her stomach, the utter revulsion shocked her back into motion and she turned around to run but what she did not expect was to see a clown standing behind her, with bright blue hair, melting skin with open wounds that had glowing embers dance around and smoke rising from his clothes. Jess tried to react but her body seemed to have shut down, she could not move or scream, and she was not necessarily sure she was even breathing.

She could not tell if he was smiling or growling as his jaw hung oddly. He stood there staring at her and Jess honestly wondered if today was the day she was going to die. She got lucky last time, maybe tonight may not be the case. Just before Jess regained herself and managed to react, the clown's arm sprang to life, grabbing her with both hands so she could not move away. The moment his hands touched, she felt this piercing heat of pain shoot through her entire body. She screamed out in blinding pain to the point she was going to pass out. She could hear the clown screaming too but his was the hollow, high pitched sound only a demon could make. Jess's body felt like it was being burnt from the inside out as her body gave into the pain, and the world around her gradually went darker.

Chapter 11

Jess awoke on the floor, but it was not her floor, she was in a field outside. When she looked up, she saw the clown staring straight at her. Without questioning how she ended up outside, she tried to rise to her feet as quickly as she could but struggled to do so, like she was moving underwater again and everything moved in slow motion. It was night-time. She could not see anything but the grass beneath her and the clown, who was still watching her. By the time she finally got up on her feet, she could see a giant big top circus tent erected behind the clown, all lit up. Trailer vans were parked around the circus and dated vehicles dotted around the field. People were now around them. They seemed unaware of the burning clown or the ragged, distressed woman. They were laughing, running, skipping and walking, but Jess did not quite understand how she knew this. None of the people were moving, they were in still frames, a tableau. Yet every time Jess took a step forward the tableau would change as if jumping forward in time. The people would seem to blur slightly and end up closer to the lit-up tent.

Jess studied their faces and their clothes, and knew she was looking in on a different decade to the one she lived in. She turned back to the clown, who was just standing there. She had just been attacked by this monster to the point of passing out but she currently felt no fear. The clown slowly moved his head and looked towards the big top, then looked back at Jess and pointed to the entrance of the circus.

Jess did not understand what was going on but she knew she was being instructed to do something. Taking advantage of her newfound bravery, she felt it best to comply. She walked towards the circus entrance, and by the time she reached the big top, like in all her dreams, the lights were off, the people were gone and she was alone. Time also once again seemed to move normally. She looked around the tent as déjà vu struck her and she saw a solitary light coming from one of the caravans. She walked towards it. As she did, she could hear sobbing coming from inside. She climbed the wooden steps that led to the door and peeped through the small, mud stained window. Two children sat on the floor. A boy and a girl. The boy was silent whilst the little girl sobbed. Jess realised she had dreamed of these children before, but what shocked her even more was that these were the children from the murder. She recognised their faces in the police report with their school pictures attached. This was a nightmare. She knew these children were going to die and there was nothing she could do about it.

"Why are you *still* crying?!" a voice boomed from a side of the caravan where Jess could not see. An object flew towards the girl's head and narrowly missed. Jess wanted to scream out and stop this, but as her mouth opened she could smell the strong stench of burning flesh surround her. She slowly turned her head and the rotting clown face was merely inches away from hers. Staring at her, he raised his finger to his mouth. She knew she was being told to stay silent.

As she turned her head back to look through the window, it felt like once again she was moving through water, and even though she had only taken her eyes away from the scene for a moment, what she now saw in the caravan needed much more time. She could see a little body lying on the floor, she could only see the feet protruded out from behind a chair. She was grateful that the rest of the body was hidden from view. There was blood everywhere. The man, who she now knew to be Billy Bob, was pacing the room rambling to himself.

"She wouldn't shut up, she wouldn't shut up, she wouldn't shut up," he repeated to himself without stopping.

Jess felt a nudge on her shoulder and turned to see David Benson, the clown, but alive and unharmed, with no makeup on. He didn't acknowledge her presence whilst simultaneously physically moving her to one side so he could get past. The burning clown stood to one side, never taking his eyes off Jess and keeping his finger to his mouth.

David burst into the caravan door and stood still momentarily before looking at the blood-stained Billy Bob.

"W...what d...d...did you...do?" David struggled to get out.

"Now, now David. I didn't want to do this, but they made me. They wouldn't shut up," he explained calmly.

"Th... th.... they're ch... chiild... dren?" David's stutter was getting stronger the more upset he clearly got.

Billy Bob walked over to David and slapped him across the face.

"I tell you what David, you're going to keep your fucking mouth shut. If you tell anyone, I'll tell them that you did it. You're the children's clown, the entertainer. You spend all day with them. The police are just going to think you've been grooming them all along and you finally snapped or some shit. Who do you think they're going to believe? The owner's son? Or the stuttering retard?"

Jess could see David was physically shaking. She couldn't tell if it was from upset, anger or fear.

"Y... y... y....." David was struggling to talk so badly he couldn't get one word out.

Jess felt suddenly dizzy, as if she was underwater again. Hearing something behind her, she turned around, the world blurring past her as she did. There before her she could now see two policemen standing outside the caravan talking to young Billy Bob, who was wearing a clean change of clothes. It was still night but Jess could only assume that this was days later.

"I wish I could help more officers. It's such a tragedy what happened. Children's faces all blur into one I'm afraid, but I do remember on that night, David, who plays the clown, was talking to a boy and girl after the show. He was making them balloon animals around the trailers. I thought it odd as the show was over, but I just assumed he knew them. He doesn't talk much because of his severe stutter and just keeps to himself a lot, ya know?" Billy Bob explained to the policeman as politely as he could. "This is his trailer, I think he's in there if you want to ask him anything."

"Thank you, we'll come back to you if we need anything. You've been most helpful." David had been pointing to the same caravan where the children were murdered. The police climbed the steps, with Jess going unnoticed yet again as they went inside. Jess could see David was sitting on the bed, and the entire caravan was clean now, no blood in sight.

"David Benson?" the first policeman addressed him sternly.

"Y...y....es?"

"I am Detective Fields and this is my partner Detective Ward. We'd like to ask you a few questions."

"S...sure."

"Where were you the night of November 12th?"

"Here. W...working." David looked shaken, his gaunt face looked more ill than ever from the stress. Jess couldn't help but feel sorry for him.

"Have you ever seen these two children?"

"No," David lied.

"We have witnesses saying they saw you talking to these children alone after the show." The first policeman, Ward, was asking all the questions whilst Jess could see the second clenching his fist.

"I d... d... didn't."

"Can we search your... accommodation?" Detective Ward asked. He seemed to struggle with his wording whilst looking around at the minimal but shoddy décor.

"O... of c... course."

The two policemen started looking around, opening cupboards, looking under cushions. Jess would lose sight of them when they wandered off to different parts of the caravan. Ward brought a heavy brown leather trunk the height of the policeman's hips on its side from an unknown location.

"Just seen this in your cupboard. What's inside? It's very heavy." David looked perplexed at the suitcase, fidgeting on the bed suddenly.

"That's n.... not m.... mine."

"It's locked, do you have the code?" Ward asked, ignoring him.

"I d... on't kn... kn... know it. It's n... not mine."

Ward grabbed a Swiss army knife from his pocket and jammed it into the suitcase slot, jiggling it until it burst open. Jess let out a gasp at the sight of two mangled corpses inside. A young boy and a girl, naked and folded into it in such an unnatural position; she could see both policemen turn green from the sight of it.

"Joe, don't look," Detective Ward said to his colleague, but it was too late, the other cop physically seemed to have gone weak from the sight of the contents inside. His lip started to quiver and he took a step towards the trunk.

"Sophie?" His voice was breaking, clearly on the edge of tears.

"Joe, don't. We got the bastard, it's all we can do now." Detective Ward tried to grab the other by the shoulders and turn him away from the sight, but Fields shook free from him.

"That's my daughter in that fucking box!" Fields screamed, pacing the room. "And you put her there!" He turned to David, spitting these words like venom at him. David looked horrified and confused.

"Th.... th.... that's...... n..... not...... m..... m..... m...." His stammer was next to impossible to understand right now, but before he could finish the sentence Detective Fields punched him so hard it knocked him flat onto the bed. Fields then got on top of him, punching him non-stop, one blow after another, alternating fists. Detective Ward eventually dragged his friend off but Fields wouldn't let go of David, grabbing him by the scruff and trying to make him stand up but he was unconscious, or near enough, so he just hung there limp on his knees, hanging from his collar that was still tightly in the grip of Fields. Jess could see his jaw hanging funny, it seemed dislocated or broken from one of the blows given to him. Jess stared back at the clown, watching how his mouth would swing ever so slightly as he still just stood there, watching her, almost like he did not care about what was happening to himself in there, or he did not want to watch.

"Joe, don't do this, we're going to throw everything we have at this fucker and he will never leave prison for the rest of his life."

"Prison is too good for him!" he screamed hysterically, tears running down his cheeks. "He killed my daughter! He killed Chris's boy! We have to live with that forever, and he, what? Gets to live?! How is that fair?" He was pleading with his friend, whilst constantly swaying and moving on the spot, he was so beside himself. He clearly had no fixed plan on what to do next. David started to groan as he gained consciousness.

"Why did you do it?" Detective Fields asked, shaking him.

"I.... d.... d.... didn't." Fields took long, slow breaths in, trying to calm down.

"You did. We have found.... the bodies." His voice broke. "Now tell me... please. Why did you kill my little girl? I need to know. Why did you take her from me?"

"I....... I....... d..... d.... d.... didn't."

"You lying piece of shit." This was said quietly by Detective Ward, who had just been staring at the trunk, looking at the mangled bodies, unnatural shapes created just to get them to fit in. Covered in blood, naked. It was too much. Ward couldn't justify trying to save his friend from the heartbreak he would hopefully never have to endure. "I'll be back in five minutes, Joe. I'm just going to get the handcuffs, I must have forgotten them." Jess could clearly see handcuffs in his hand but she had gathered that was not the real reason he was leaving. Fields must have known that too, because the second Ward had left and closed the door behind him, he did not stop punching him, he punched David in the nose - which caused an explosion of blood - he punched him in the jaw, eyes, cheeks... everywhere. He dropped him to the floor and started to kick as hard as he could into his stomach, legs and back. David threw up but it did not stop Fields, he just kept kicking him as hard as his steel toe capped boots would allow. Jess could hear ribs crack with every blow to them, she heard the bones crunching when the policeman stood on David's fingers, breaking every one. Jess knew he was innocent, the only person in the world except for the clown himself, and her heart was breaking and her stomach felt sick.

In just the space of a couple of minutes, by the time Ward returned, David was unrecognisable. Fields was standing over him panting, out of breath, whilst David's face was already swollen and bloody. He was struggling to move with so many broken bones. Ward was momentarily horrified but then said quietly: "It won't be the last beating he gets, I'll make sure the whole prison knows about him and what he did."

David started to whimper and cry, his bloodied and tangled fingers tried to reach for something sturdy to help pull him up and get away from the policeman.

"I.... d...... d..... d..... didn't..... do...... it."

Even after everything, the evidence, the beating, the fact David was still denying the crime should have been enough to make a policeman question if they did in fact have the wrong man, but it simply angered them even more. The fact this low life would have the audacity to try and lie to the grieving father of a murdered child seemed to send them both over the edge. They both screamed at him in anger and started to kick him again. David screamed and tried to crawl away. He reached for anything in front of him with his mutilated fingers, which happened to be a small table by the side of his bed. As he pulled on it, it toppled over, making everything on top of it fall around him, including an oil lamp he had lit earlier that evening. The oil sprayed all over him, blistering his skin instantly. He screamed in agony, louder than before, Fields kicked him in the jaw to shut up him, cutting his tongue between his teeth. David was unconscious again. The police watched as the flame from the oil burner quickly set the old, dry carpet alight and the flames began to reach the curtains. Embers were starting to singe and crawl onto David's clothes. The policemen made no effort to stop the burning. They stood there momentarily debating whether to save him or not.

"His body is banged up pretty bad Andrew, far worse than I could explain away as self-defence or resisting arrest," Fields explained to Ward.

"You did do a number on him... I... I shouldn't have left." Ward looked guilty, he had allowed emotion to take priority over justice in the eyes of the law.

"You gave me something I needed Andrew, closure. That fucker deserved every painful moment I just put him through."

The fire started to spread at an alarming rate. they turned around to see that most of the caravan was in flames now. They needed to leave. Ward went to grab David's feet but then stopped, turned around and helped Fields carry the heavy trunk out first. As Fields carried out his dead daughter he stared at the flaming caravan around him and muttered, more to himself than anyone else.

"It wasn't enough."

By the time they climbed down the small steps and put the trunk away at a safe distance, the caravan collapsed on itself, making it impossible to save David even if they wanted to. The two policemen stood there, silent, regretting nothing.

Jess didn't remember moving, but she was now standing closer to the big top, watching the caravan burn down from a safer distance, knowing an innocent man just died. Her eyes watered and stung from the smoke. She turned to look at the clown, who still never took his eyes off her. He then pointed at a different caravan. She looked over. It was slightly bigger than David's was but much cleaner, clearly well taken care of and possibly new. She turned around to look back at the old caravan and no police were to be seen, no fire burning away and the clown's caravan was gone, like it had never even existed. Turning back to the new caravan in question, she started to walk towards it once again, feeling like she was going through water. With every step the world around her would blur, and when it was back in focus things would have changed slightly. By the time she reached the caravan it was daylight, and she recognised a car parked outside being close to a model of her own. The door of the caravan swung open before she got close enough to be in the way and the Ringmaster, as she knew him today, walked out. Buttoning up his shirt and walking towards the tent. This was his caravan. Jess climbed the steps and, feeling a little braver but hoping no one was in there, tried the door handle. It opened, and as she stepped in she almost screamed at the sight of the clown who was already waiting inside for her. Everything was so clean and modern inside. Simple. But modern. There was a small TV propped up in the dining part where a clean and well-sprung couch spread from one side to another and even wrapped around the corners. She leaned over a newspaper on the table and read the date, it was dated three days ago. The circus was in her town right now, in the present. She turned to look down the other side of the caravan and the clown was already waiting for her at the far end by a door. She walked down, and when she opened the door there was a small bedroom. The room was just big enough to fit a bed and set of drawers in. Jess looked back, perhaps for some sort of guidance, but the clown was gone. She looked down and jumped at the sight of a hand so thin it reminded her of a skeleton with crooked fingers stretched out from the under the bed, waving her down to look closer. She got on her knees and looked under the bed. There was nothing under there except the clown, lying flat on his stomach, staring at her. There was no more than a three inch gap from the floor to the bed, yet he managed to fit underneath rather comfortably. He waved his hand again, signalling for her to join him and, without questioning it, Jess tried to join him. The gap under the bed seemed to grow to accommodate her, growing so much she could even crawl on her knees and not on her stomach. When reaching the clown he pointed to the floor. There was a tear in the carpet. Jess pulled at it. Underneath was a loose wooden frame. Jess tried to get her fingers inside and pull it out; it was stiff but moveable and eventually she managed it. With one board out of the way she could see something was below. She pulled up more boards until she realised it was a suitcase lying beneath them. The same leather colour of the trunk that Billy Bob had hid the bodies in. She pulled it out and opened it. Inside were seven items. A little doll which looked dirty and old. A pink comb, a football sticker book dated 1985, a sock with yellow frills on the end, a blue dress, a brown t-shirt and a pair of large, thick rimmed glasses. Jess's blood felt like it had turned solid and refused to pump through her body when she realised all the clothes were children's sizes. What made her feel nauseous though was she recognised the dress and t-shirt. They were the same clothes the boy and girl were wearing when they were murdered. The murder that David was framed for.

"He kept these..." Jess stated out loud, then, remembering the date on the newspaper. "He *still* has these." The clown slowly nodded his head, confirming what she said. Jess stared at the burning clown. He was a terrifying sight, but she started to realise he was not evil. He was framed. The charismatic Ringmaster was the evil and terrifying one, and he was getting away with it.

The clown tilted his head and then pressed his hand on her arm. For a split second she felt the intense and excruciating pain run through her arm. She closed her eyes and screamed in agony once again.

Chapter 12

"Jess, it's ok, it's ok, I'm here, I'm here." Jess opened her eyes, startled to hear the sound of Matt's voice. She looked up to find she was lying on the floor of her living room in Matt's arms, who was on his knees. She sat up, moving her head around, checking to see if she felt like she was underwater and was dreaming. She looked around for a clown, frantically checking to see if she was still holding the children's clothes. She would have sworn she was under the Ringmaster's bed, clutching at such horrifying evidence only a moment ago... but they were no longer there. Nothing was.

"Are you there?" Jess asked Matt quizzically.

"Am I what?"

"Are you real?"

"Of course I am."

"How did you get here? I told you to go home."

"Jess, I was only down the drive, I could hear your scream from there. I ran back but the door was locked and you were still screaming. I called the police and I knocked your door in. When I got through you were passed out on the floor, shaking. No matter how much I tried to shake you or wake you, you didn't respond. You were only out for like five or 10 minutes but it was pretty scary, Jess."

It took several minutes for Jess to calm down and to realise that she was no longer dreaming. Once she had calmed down, she thanked Matt, hugging him and finally giving in to being vulnerable around him. He held her tight whilst they sat on the couch and she told him everything she saw, everything she had researched and all about the clown again. Matt did not know how to respond. He wanted to believe it was all due to stress and visions, but he had to admit, if Jess was telling the truth about everything, some things did not rationally add up as neatly as he would like.

Since Matt had phoned the police earlier on, the police came round to check out that everything was ok. Besides a very messy living room, Jess insisted that she was fine and Matt seemed a lot calmer than he did on the phone so they did not stay for too long. As they were walking out, curiosity got the better of them and they had to question the paper display scattered around her living room. She lied and said it was research for school since the class trip was to go to the circus. They seemed satisfied by that response and left thinking nothing more of the event.

"If you genuinely believe that this man is a murderer, who still keeps some sort of trophies from a murder that happened forever ago, why didn't you tell the police? Ask them to check it out?" Matt quizzed.

"Because they already think I'm a bit of an unstable person since the clown broke into my house and I was adamant it wasn't human. How is it going to sound when I say excuse me Mr policeman, but I think a ghost gave me a vision of himself being framed for a murder he didn't commit and the evidence for it is hiding under the Ringmaster's bed? I'll tell you what they won't do; check the circus, and I'll tell you what they will do, make sure I never teach their children again."

"If you know it sounds so crazy, why do you believe it so much? You're a smart woman, you know how brains can play tricks, how real dreams can seem, smell things that aren't there."

"Because..." Jess started with a sigh, tired of explaining herself. "Because I'm not crazy, I genuinely thought I was for a moment, I won't lie, and I know this..." she waved her hands, gesturing towards all the paper "...doesn't help my sanity plea, but I know what I experienced. I know what I felt. I know what I saw. I know it's real, Matt. I dreamt of people, faces, clothes and events before I knew they were even real. I genuinely did believe they were just nightmares, but then I researched it and saw the same faces in my dreams printed out in police reports."

"If you genuinely believe it's the truth, you should tell the police, they will find the truth."

"They will do nothing with the fact there is no evidence except a dream I had. It will end up with everyone thinking I'm crazy and me getting even more crazy and sympathetic looks in the staff room, and that's if I even get to keep my job."

"So what are you going to do?"

"The only thing I can do, I'm going to get that suitcase." Jess had started to move about frantically, cleaning up the paper, drawing from memory the layout of how the circus had been pitched.

"What?!"

"The circus is only here for two more nights, including this one. I'm going to go and get that suitcase and prove that they got the wrong murderer all those years ago."

"That's the most insane thing I've ever heard. It's illegal, it's breaking and entering, you will definitely lose your job over that," Matt explained while Jess ignored him, keeping her eyes fixated on what she was drawing.

"I watched an innocent man beaten and burnt to death." She made another attempt at drawing a map. "Some things are more important."

"Why you? Why no one else?" Jess had wondered this herself. She folded up the paper, got up, grabbed a coat and was trying to find her shoes. Getting changed into normal clothes did not seem to have crossed her mind.

"I think it's because I've seen him before. When I was a child. All the other reports I found who said they saw this clown were all children under 13. Maybe only children can see him. Maybe he's asking for help. Maybe he's saving us in his mind by taking us away from the circus. Maybe that's why I can still see him and no one else can. No one believed me when I was seven, I grew up being victim blamed for something I told the truth about. Do you know how much therapy my parents forced me to have? They blamed themselves, nearly got divorced, sometimes they didn't even like being around me. They would never say, but I knew. We used to be such a loving family but it was never the same after the circus. That's why they moved to London, I think they hate being alone together, they'll just fight again over who is the worst parent, and I hate being around them, because I still feel like it's my fault. I never expected anyone to believe me this time but what's worse, you all started to make me doubt myself. Question if I was in fact going crazy. I'm doing this because I have to prove to myself that I am sane, and when I was seven, I was sane too."

"Jess, I can't let you do this. I can't help you do this. This is illegal." Matt stared at her pleadingly. Jess slowed down and sat heavily onto the couch.

"I never asked you to come with me, but I am going. I need to do this. I will never get over this horror if I don't. It is something I have to do and you can not stop me, so please, don't try." Jess fell silent as Matt held her hand loosely in his. He was trying to think of something he could say or do that could distract her for long enough until she calmed down and realised she could not really go through with this.

"At least put on some warmer clothes. Stained pyjamas aren't really what 007 would wear," he tried to joke. Jess smiled, nodded her head and looked down at her attire.

"You're probably right. Ok, I will get dressed first, but I mean it Matt, you can't stop me, I'm going back to that circus. Tonight."

Chapter 13

Parked outside the circus, Jess sat in her car. Silently she watched as the breath visibly danced around, reminding her too much of her dreams. Her hands clutched the steering wheel for support. Every time she let go she could see her fingers shaking from adrenaline and fear. Her mouth was dry and she was suddenly aware of how heavy she was breathing.

"You can do this," she said out loud in a voice that did not match the confidence of her words.

She had decided it best to park down the very end of the field carpark, as far from the circus as she could. She was worried about parking her car there at all, in case it drew attention to herself. But then she remembered that when she came here, she was in the school bus. No one knew her car to recognise her. Besides, the field was so dark and badly lit that nobody would be able to see her car all the way from the white picket fence that marked the beginning of the actual circus area anyway. For now, she was safe. She had no solid plan and no real idea of how she was going to get that suitcase. She just knew that she had to get it. She was very aware that she was dealing with someone who had taken more than one life in the past, but she also hoped that in his old age he was slow and weak if anything physical took place. She needed to be safe and smart. It was 9pm. The final show had just started and was due to finish at 10:30pm. Most of the staff and entertainers would be busy around this time, and she felt this was her best chance to get to his caravan without being seen. She got the crude map she had drawn out and examined it one more time. She had to go past the big top to get to the caravan quickly. She could either go left, around the back of the big top, which was slower but there were far less people and caravans there, or she could go straight past the entrance, which was quicker but would mean she had to go past a lot more caravans that could have people in them. Either way was a gamble.

She got out of the car and tried to walk as calmly and as normal as possible, but she was very conscious of the fact her legs did not seem to move the way they normally did. Her feet felt heavier with every step until she felt so weighed down she questioned if she was dreaming again. She was so used to seeing the red and white big top, the flashing lights, the smell of stale popcorn and hot dogs that it was strange to think she had actually only been here once with the school trip. Twice if you included when she was seven.

By the time she made it to the white picket fence she had to decide which direction to go; left, the quieter but slower route that took her around the back of the big top, or right, past the entrance and through the caravans, which was much more direct but ran a much higher risk of getting caught.

She settled on going right. Her logic behind this was, if she got caught going around the back, she would struggle to explain why she was there. It would be very clear she was doing something she should not be doing and she could find herself in danger. Going right, walking straight past the entrance and getting 'lost' seemed much more of a plausible excuse to her. There were two adults standing by the entrance having a cigarette but she could not see anyone who seemed to be staff, working there. She kept telling herself if she walked with a purpose, like she knew what she was doing, no one would question her. She was so grateful she had actually changed clothes before coming out. Walking around in pyjamas would definitely have not been the inconspicuous look she was going for. As she approached the entrance, she realised the adults standing by the entrance smoking were parents of two of the children she taught in her class.

"Fuck!" she internally hissed to herself. She was right in the open and she could not turn back now, it was too obvious and there was nowhere else to go but straight; she hoped it was too dark or they were too involved with their own conversation to notice her. She kept her head low and tried to walk at a pace that would not draw any attention to herself. For a second she thought she had made eye contact with one of the ladies, but no one said anything. She forced herself to keep her eyes straight ahead. With her heart in her throat she was almost past the entrance and about to turn the corner when she heard: "Miss Befria! What are you doing here? I've heard you've been off. Are you ok?"

"Fuck fuck fuck fuck fuck," Jess screamed in her head. She stood frozen for a second, debating how to respond. The longer she stood by the entrance, the more likely it was that someone would see her, and her only opportunity would be gone, forever. She also could not just run away without saying anything. She had to address them, but she had to make it quick. She took a deep breath and with the most fake smile she could manage, turned around to face the small group.

"Mrs Peters, Miss Robinson, nice to see you! Yes, I've been terribly ill lately; thankfully though, all better and back on Monday. I'm just here talking to the circus about some mementos we could keep from the school trip we had. Carl and Suzy especially loved the trip, did they tell you that? They were so good, you wouldn't have even known they were there. Well look at that, I just can't keep up with the time, I must run, I'll see you on Monday, enjoy the show, it's brilliant." Jess rapidly walked past the exit and kept walking until she was around the side of the tent and out of sight of the nosey parents. Her legs felt numb and she was struggling to breathe. She completely over-explained everything and realised just how strange and crazy she must have come across, but she had no time to chat and be polite. The longer she stood by the entrance, the more likely someone from the circus would have noticed her, maybe even Billy Bob himself. She looked straight ahead of herself and a few feet in front of her was the caravan she recognised.

"I knew I wasn't making this up," she thought, smiling to herself. Her pace quickened as she kept darting back and forth to see if anyone was around...

No one...

She jumped up the metal steps and went to the door. She tried to press her ear to it just in case anyone was inside, but she heard nothing. She touched the door and opened it. She was grateful it was not locked... she had not really planned for that, and would not have had a clue what to do. She threw herself in and shut the door behind her.

The inside was exactly how she dreamt it. Everything was minimal, but clean and fairly new. She turned and went to the little door on the left she knew to be the bedroom. Even though the front door was not locked, this one was.

"Well, a murderer would have to make sure incriminating evidence would be safe... Fuck!" Jess looked at the lock; it was a little Yale style lock fitted in the handle itself. She remembered seeing the police open the trunk by sticking a knife in and thought maybe she could do the same, but then remembered the policeman probably knew what he was doing. Then it happened; she could smell burning hair and flesh. She panicked for a second and her heart stopped. She turned around to see Peekaboo, the clown, staring at her. She went to scream. She would never get used to his appearance, but then she also remembered, he wasn't the bad guy now. Billy Bob was. The clown pointed to a drawer next to her, attached to an area designated to being the kitchen. She opened it to see knives and forks, a tin opener, bottle opener and other utilities you would expect to need when cooking. She was starting to get confused but then she saw a little tin, almost like an old-fashioned pillbox about the size of a match box. She opened it and inside were two keys. Her eyes lit up and she poured them both out into her hand. She tried the first one into the lock, twisted it and nothing happened. Feeling disheartened she put the first key to one side and trying again she picked up the second key and went to insert it. Her hands shook so violently she actually struggled to find the keyhole, but she eventually managed it, turned the key, and voila, the door unlocked. She stepped inside the tiny room, frantically got to her knees and looked under the bed. She struggled to see but knew she could not turn any of the lights on, that would be far too obvious. She tried to slip her arm underneath the bed and feel for a tear in the carpet, it was a tight fit but eventually she felt the stray fibres between her fingers, she pulled and felt the carpet easily come away from the floor. That was the spot. She grabbed the base of the bed, pulled it up and tried to rest it on its side. The pillows went flying but she did not care right now, she felt for the lip in the carpet again and when she found it, tore at it eagerly, revealing the wooden panels. She struggled initially as she fingered the grooves, trying to get leverage, but eventually a board gave in and popped out. The rest of the boards popped out too, one by one. After she removed four boards she could see, underneath, was a dark brown suitcase. Jess lost her ability to breathe for a second and the realisation hit her that this was all real.

She pulled the dusty suitcase out and whilst on her knees, rested the suitcase on her legs and opened it. Inside were the exact pink comb, sticker book, sock, dress, t-shirt and glasses that she had seen in her dream. The smell of dust and mould violently rose from the suitcase and filled the room.

"I can't believe it. It's true," Jess said out loud in disbelief.

"I can't believe it either," said a booming voice behind her. Jess spun around and saw a dark figure standing in the doorway. The figure flipped a switch to turn the light on, and Jess realised it was Billy Bob himself. His dark eyes stared down at her, his expression displayed silent rage. She could not wake up out of this nightmare. Her heart dropped into her stomach.

"It's very rude to break into someone's living accommodation, you know? What do people teach kids these days?" he said, almost teasingly. He did not even sound mad as he slowly walked up to her until he was towering over her as she was still on her knees. He stood there staring for a few moments, not saying a single word, and Jess, frozen, could not think of what she could say to help her. Jess's heart was beating so hard she was convinced Billy Bob would be able to hear it himself. Suddenly, and without hesitation, he pounced like a feral animal. His hands wrapped tightly around her neck. She tried to scream but she could not breathe, she tried to grab at his fingers and pry them off but through absolute panic she could not coordinate her fingers to save her life. She tried to kick out and hurt him but could not seem to hit him. A sudden ringing in her ears became painfully loud and she could not hear anything. She could feel her pulse through her neck and up to her temples. Her vision turned from clear to blurry.

Then all she saw was black.

Chapter 14

Jess's eyes slowly opened, adjusting to the light around her. Her throat was sore and she was lying on the ground. She went to move but realised she was tied up and her mouth was gagged. Panic started to set in. She looked around her and could see that she was still in Billy Bob's bedroom in the caravan. The bed was still lifted and on its side, resting against the wall. Next to her was the open suitcase. All the contents still remained in there. Billy Bob was nowhere to be seen. She tried to calm her breathing and strain her ears for any noise coming from unseen rooms. For now, she was alone and she started to cry. When Billy Bob had started to choke her, she was convinced her time had ran out and she was going to die there and then. Waking up again from that horrific blackout made her value life more than she thought possible. She could not stop berating herself for going about everything the wrong way, being so fixated on gaining closure, and how idiotic it was of her to come here alone. She heard footsteps outside and her body started to shake. She listened as they kicked dirt on the ground and how the metal steps creaked under the weight of someone climbing them to enter the caravan. She heard the steps grow louder as they came into the room, and then she cried more when she saw it was Billy Bob, probably here to finish what he had started. He stood there watching her calmly as he leaned on the door frame. For someone who had just choked a human unconscious and tied them up, he was still immaculately dressed in his Ringmaster's clothing.

"I hope I didn't keep you waiting long. You see I was in the middle of a show before and I only returned because my shirt had gotten stained and I needed a new one. Doesn't happen often, but what a shame for you it did tonight." He moved closer, then, kneeling over her, grabbed Jess's shoulders and sat her up. He moved his face closer to hers. Horror struck her for a second; he got so close she thought he was going to kiss her. "You would have gotten away by now otherwise." His breath was hot and smelt of stale cigarettes. She could see his crooked yellowed teeth and his thin, wrinkled lips curl into a smile. Her stomach dropped. She tried to talk, but the makeshift gag of cloth was shoved so deep into her mouth that every time she moved to speak it would make her gag and choke. He watched her struggle to breathe whilst his cold dark eyes seemed to glisten. He tilted his head slightly and then slowly moved the gag.

"Be warned. If you scream. I will kill you right now, on the spot, and judging from what you were looking for, you know I will."

Jess's body grew stiff from fear, but she managed to nod her head to show she understood the severity of the situation. She had so much she wanted to ask about the murders, she had so much she wanted to accuse him of, but above all she just wanted to beg for her life. Before she could decide on what to say, Billy Bob had leaned back and sat on the floor, leaning against the wall opposite her. Only now Jess realised he was holding a knife in his right hand, and Jess thought begging might actually be the best option.

"Now, I'm going to ask you a few questions. If you lie to me, I will hurt you. Do you understand?" he asked calmly. Jess nodded in agreement as tears fell down her face. "Why were you looking for that suitcase?" Jess did not know how to answer that, but she knew there was no lie she could tell that would ever make sense.

"Because.... because I knew what was inside it." Jess could not think of any other way to word it.

"Did you now?" he inquired. He sounded intrigued in a mocking way, like he was humouring her. "Do you know what the objects are? What they mean?"

"I think so..." Jess contemplated risking everything and screaming as loud as she could, hoping that someone would be outside and hear, but she knew it would mean her life if nobody was. She was aware that admitting she knew he was a murderer would mean that she would never leave this caravan alive. She could see him trying to balance the tip of the knife on the floor whilst holding the handle; every now and again the blade would catch the light and shine over Jess's face.

"And what do you think it means?" he asked.

"That you killed those two children." Jess felt a little braver saying these words. She believed she was the first person to ever say them to him. She imagined catching him off guard, and being the morally superior being, she would talk him down into seeing the error of his ways, he would untie her and turn himself in and she would live a happy life never getting involved in anyone's business ever again. Jess's daydream was killed when she saw him chuckling to himself.

"Only two eh? Each trinket is a trophy. I may not have killed every one of them but I also know what I am doing. Miss Befria, I know how to make it painless, but I also know how to make it very, very painful." Jess's mouth fell open in disbelief as he recognised her.

"I remember you from the school trip," he explained. "You seemed so quiet and reserved in the circus. I thought you seemed suspicious of me even then but no, your colleagues just assured me you were terrified of circuses and so I thought nothing more of it. I do come across coulrophobia from time to time... never a phobia of a circus in general though. Until I saw you looking at the photographs. The questions you were asking made you stand out. Quite a pretty face to forget anyway, should I add." He twisted his head from staring at the knife to her, stretching those thin lips across his face into a repulsive, yellow toothed smile. Jess felt her skin crawl in disgust.

"You've murdered more?"

"Enough. People who get in my way. You're not the first person to come looking for this suitcase." This piece of information shocked Jess at first, but then she remembered Peter Neil and his blog post. There could have even been more who just never wrote about it.

"Really? When? How did they know?" Jess blurted out, without thinking.

"He was not as talkative as you I'm afraid. He never said. But he seemed to know exactly where to look as well, so I gather you both found out the same way. So whatever little rumour is flying around, I will find the source of it and quench it. And you, Miss Befria, will tell me. I got impatient with the other one, just snapped his neck, which I suppose was lucky for him." Billy Bob moved his hands over the suitcase and picked up the glasses. He looked at them with a disturbingly warm look. As if he were looking at a memento from a happy summer holiday he experienced in his childhood. He then stopped smiling and looked at Jess with his cold, hard eyes. "You will tell me, however, or you will suffer." Jess began to cry uncontrollably. She knew she was going to die and it was going to be painfully. "How did you find out about that suitcase?" he asked calmly.

"You wouldn't believe me."

"Try me."

"I dreamt it."

Billy Bob, who had resumed playing with the knife, stopped momentarily and looked at her.

"You dreamt it? You expect me to believe that?"

"It is the truth!" Jess screamed. Considering Billy Bob must be in his early 60s, Jess, was amazed at the speed he jumped across the room and slapped her hard across the face.

"You raise your voice like that again, I'll cut your tongue out." He stood over her, he spoke calmly and monotonously but she could see his fists shaking with adrenaline and anger.

"It's the truth," she whimpered.

"I'm a fair man, but not a patient one. I can see you're not going to tell me." He started to pace the room, looked at his watch and groaned. "I have to go back to work. When I get back, you have one chance to tell me the truth. If you don't, I'm done playing. I will hurt you. I will make you suffer more pain than you can handle. Then I will kill you. So think about that." He scooped down and grabbed the gag, shoving it back in her mouth whilst Jess tried to struggle away from it, begging the entire time not to have it placed back in her mouth.

He left the room, turning the light off again whilst shutting the bedroom door, and moments later she heard the front door shut too. She was alone, she was tied up and she was going to die.

Chapter 15

Jess sat there in the darkness, in a frenzy of panic. She had no idea how long he would be but she could not sit around waiting to find out. Her wrists were tied behind her back and no matter how much she wriggled, the rope would not loosen. Same for her feet. She tried to fall onto the ground and squirm and do as many awkward shapes as she could think of to try and move forwards towards the door, but nothing worked, she was stuck.

As she lay there, simultaneously trying to come up with a plan but to also stay brave, she heard shuffling about outside. She froze and listened to try and figure out if it was Billy Bob returning.

"Jess?" she heard a voice whisper outside. "Jess, are you in there?" Her heart soared as she realised it was Matt and then quickly sank as she could not do anything to get his attention. She looked to see how far away she was from the outside wall and tried to reach it, stretching her legs. She was too far away. She tried crawling and wriggling like her life depended on it, and somehow she managed to get close enough so she could kick the wall as hard as she could manage. She screamed as loud as she could through the cloth gag, still choking and gagging every other moment whilst relentlessly kicking on the wall, hoping Matt would hear it and understand the signal.

"Jess? Is that you?" he whispered again.

Luckily, somehow through all the screaming and movement, the gag actually became loose. She threw her head from side to side and she tried to spit the cloth out, which she eventually managed.

"Matt! Help!" she screamed. There was no hesitation. Seconds later, Jess heard the front door to the caravan crash open and feet stomping quickly towards her, the door flew open, the light flickered on and he stared in horror at Jess on the floor.

"Grab a knife in the kitchen, hurry!" Jess instructed. Matt was gone for only a minute but she could not stop crying, she was so terrified of being so close to escaping just to be caught again. He flew in with a serrated knife and started to saw at the rope. It was taking a while as the rope was pretty thick, but they eventually managed to cut through it. Jess rubbed her sore wrists as they were about to leave. As they began to move Jess stopped abruptly, turning around.

"Wait, I'm not going without this." She ran back into the room, closed the suitcase and picked it up. With the suitcase in hand she turned to leave, but what she saw next made her heart stop. There, in the doorway, was Matt being held with a knife to his neck and Billy Bob walking in, holding the knife.

"Well, I guess you little fuckers just don't like to listen. Running away before it was my turn to play... that just isn't fair," Billy Bob said sinisterly.

"Let him go, he doesn't know anything," she pleaded, tears streaming down her face.

"Oh, but he does." Billy Bob corrected. "He knew you were here, and when you go missing, he will tell people that. So now, he has to go missing too."

Billy Bob slowly took a step or two towards Jess whilst still holding the blade to Matt's throat. Suddenly, Jess could smell burning hair and rotting flesh. She looked over Billy Bob's shoulders and saw the clown in the corner of the room. Smoke was rising from him thicker than she had ever seen, and flames were bursting from his clothes and his flesh, like his lungs were bellows fuelling the fire. It was hard to tell any expression on a half-melted clown face, but Jess could clearly see the look of pure hatred as he stared at the true murderer in the room.

"Wait, before you do anything, I swear, I dreamt it! All because of that clown standing behind you," Jess pleaded, pointing hysterically at the corner where the clown was standing. Billy Bob looked confused.

"There are no clowns in this circus."

"There used to be..." Jess continued. "You framed one, with blue hair, and painted hands on his face. His name was David Benson and he was beaten and burnt to death. You hid the two bodies in his caravan and you let him die. Not everyone can see him, but I can, and he is standing behind you." Jess had tears in her eyes, she did not know what was going to happen, she just did not want her or Matt to die. Billy Bob looked noticeably unsettled from all of this.

"You've told me nothing you couldn't have researched." Billy Bob seemed determined not to fall for some prank.

"When you murdered those two children, you called David a stuttering retard," Jess confirmed with a solid voice as she straightened her back. Billy Bob's face went a shade paler than it already was and sweat formed above his brow.

"...how do you know that?" he asked.

"I saw it. I saw it all. I dreamt everything, and I think David Benson is the one who showed me."

"He's dead, you just said so yourself." Billy Bob was shifting from one foot to another, becoming increasingly more nervous and wanting to look behind him but not wanting to take his eyes off Jess or Matt.

"He may be dead, but he is here; can't you smell that?"

"Smell what?" Billy Bob asked.

"Burning hair," she said sadly. The room temperature was rapidly increasing. Billy Bob tried to discreetly sniff, but Jess noticed it. What she also noticed on his face was that he could indeed smell it. It may not have been as strong for him as it was for her, but it was there, lingering in his nostrils. The curiosity got the better of him and he turned around. He looked at both corners, and just as he was about to say "There's nothing there," Jess crashed into him, knocking the knife away from Matt's throat. Billy Bob swung his heavy fist and it hit her hard in the jaw, sending her flying backwards. Matt, now free, saw this act of violence against Jess and swung back to hit Billy Bob, knocking him on the floor. The clown, invisible to all but Jess, was still there, staring, smoke rising up more than ever. Billy Bob managed to get on his feet and punched Matt back. His thick arms and wide fist dealt a crushing blow and knocked Matt onto the bed. Billy Bob dragged him by his feet onto the floor. He then started to kick Matt as hard as he could in his back. Jess looked desperately over to what she could do, and then saw the clown pointing to the cupboard beside her. She opened it - it was just a closet full of cleaning supplies. She did not understand why the clown would be pointing there, until she saw the lighter fuel and cooking matches on the shelf below.

Matt was still on the floor, close to unconscious, whilst Billy Bob was fixated on making this man feel as much pain as possible. He was so engrossed in making sure Matt would not be able to get back on his feet he failed to notice straight away that he was now covered in a heavy, foul smelling liquid. He was soaked, and the liquid felt cold but smelt strong. He looked over to Jess, who was holding the lighter fluid can. Now that she had his attention, she grabbed hold of the matches, frantically taking one out and holding it next to the strike pad.

"Let him go."

"Or what, you'll kill me?"

"I have no intention of becoming a murderer today, but if it's a simple case of us or you, I will pick us." Jess roughly rubbed the match against the match, creating a few sparks that flew from the box. Billy Bob's face dropped, unable to read Jess's body language to see if she was bluffing and unable to decide on what his next move should be.

"If I let you go, you're going to want to take that suitcase with you, aren't you?"

"Yes," Jess said, not taking her eyes off the murderer.

"You may as well kill me, then. I'm not spending the remainder of my days stuck in a prison cell. Do you know what they do to people who hurt kids?"

"Prison is too good for you!" Everyone froze. A ghostly voice screamed those words, and no one could place where they had come from, except Jess. As Billy Bob went pale as he recognised the voice, Matt seized the opportunity to crawl over to Jess. Billy Bob kept turning, frantically looking around the caravan to discover the location of the voice. The entire clown was on fire now, standing directly behind the Ringmaster, enraged at seeing the lack of justice carried out on the man who'd wronged him. He seemed to have grown in size and the smoke was so thick now Jess was coughing. Jess felt the room become so hot, a sauna would seem cold in comparison. The box of matches all seemed to ignite at once and, instinctively, Jess dropped them out of her hand. The matches landed on the floor and ignited a small lighter fuel-soaked spot on the carpet. Embers erupted from the small flame, which would light the next small puddle of lighter fuel, and that would light the next one, and so on. Like dominoes being tipped and falling one after another, all racing up the trail that led to the fuel-soaked man who was not even aware this was happening as he was desperately searching the room for David Benson. Soon, it was too late though. Billy Bob felt something hot at his feet, and as he looked down he saw the flames engulf him in one quick flash. He screamed in agony and flailed his arms about. Jess wasted no time, she grabbed the suitcase, put Matt under her arms and they limped away outside as quickly as they could manage, away from the caravan.

People ran to the caravan to inspect the screams, and when they saw the flames, ran for more help and started to call the emergency services. No one seemed to notice the two limping people running away from the flaming trailer.

Jess got Matt into the car, helping him as carefully and as quickly as she could. She then ran round to her side, desperately trying to fit the key into the keyhole. She finally got the car moving and never looked back once as she drove out of the carpark, ignoring the screams she could hear in the background. She drove faster than she ever allowed the car to go, towards the police station. She would turn the suitcase in, which would hopefully prove David Benson as an innocent man and then Jess could finally find closure from this nightmare. She turned to look at Matt. He had come to save her, he almost died for her. He sat uncomfortably in the chair, groaning constantly whilst holding his ribs.

She turned to face the road, not allowing herself to slow down or stop for anything. The sooner this chapter of her life was over, the sooner she could enjoy her future.

Chapter 16

"Can you pass me the coffee please?" Jess asked, smiling at Matt over the kitchen table while eating breakfast. He poured her a coffee, made from freshly ground beans, and pushed it along the table so their hands would touch in the middle slightly. She smiled, smelt the intoxicating aroma in her cup and went back to reading the paper.

Today was such a special day for her. For them. The headlines read '40 year old cold case solved by local teacher.'

Her mind rushed back to that night at the circus three months ago. The police had not taken any notice of her at first, believing her to be hysterical and unstable, but eventually they did look into it and had to admit it was looking suspicious. Jess had told them everything that sounded sane, including all the research she had uncovered, including the blog post of Peter Neil, who had never been discovered. With all this information, including the suitcase and a couple of other things they had on file or discovered through investigating it recently, they eventually sent it all to Kent, where the original murder had taken place. It took a couple of months but eventually Jess was notified that she was indeed correct and they now knew that David Benson was innocent and Billy Bob was indeed the murderer. Somehow, Billy Bob had survived the flames. He had been placed under arrest but was still in an intensive care unit for first degree burns on 70% of his body. Jess was grateful he did not die, she had been so terrified she would have got blamed for his death, but even the police had consoled her, explaining it would have all been in self-defence, which she had the bruises around her neck to prove.

In the past three months she had also not had a single nightmare, and she could not remember the last time she felt at such peace. She was happy.

They never knew how the match box ignited, they never asked too much about it.

"Maybe David Benson was so close to being set free, he had to help," they would half joke.

"Maybe seeing the suitcase and the clothes genuinely somehow pushed him over the edge?"

They'd try to rationalise it all but they knew, they would never really know, but Jess was ok with that.

The one thing they did know, was that all David must have wanted was for people to know the truth. And now they did.

"I better get ready for school," Jess said smiling, standing up and kissing Matt on the way out. She climbed the stairs and went into the bathroom. Stripping down, she stepped into the shower and started to wash herself. As she scrubbed her hair with shampoo, she could not stop replaying moments of the past three months. Seeing the headline today had stirred up so many emotions. Her parents had driven up the moment they heard, completely beside themselves with guilt. They still did not believe the ghost clown, but Jess suspected no one really did, maybe even Matt, who was closest to experiencing him than anyone else. Her parents, however, felt guilty for nearly losing their daughter recently and almost 20 years ago. They blamed themselves over and over to the point Jess completely forgave them on the condition they never brought it up again. After a week of tears and apologies, they went back home to London. As much as Jess loved them, she was glad to have her own space back.

Matt had pretty much been living with her the past three months. The night of the circus, Matt had later explained he found her because of one of the terribly drawn maps she had left on the coffee table. After the fire and their escape, they had gone straight to the police station and then to the hospital to check no internal injuries had taken place and to also record all the bodily harm they had received at the hands of Billy Bob. Jess could not bear the thought of spending the night alone, and truth be told, neither could Matt, so without either one of them explaining anything, Matt went back with Jess. That night, almost the moment they realised they were safe and alone, they had kissed for the very first time. Once their lips had touched, something awoke within them and they could not stop. The adrenaline pumping through their bodies from the fear of nearly dying mixed with the sheer thrill they survived, intoxicating them into a frenzy. Their first kiss was also the first time they made love, and they lay naked together for hours, holding each other in silence. Neither being able to sleep.

Everything progressed so organically for them after that, they had been through so much together. Dee was distraught when she heard about what had happened to Jess, she had visited every night for a month, just bringing everyday items round that could help her best friend. When Jess confessed what had happened between her and Matt, Dee waved her hands as if she was trying to waft the information away.

"Sweetie, you and Matt had chemistry, real chemistry from day one. Why do you think I backed off so quickly? It was obvious, you two were meant to be," Dee had explained sincerely.

Jess had been the centre of unwanted attention for the entire three months. Everyone in school, including the parents, had wanted to talk to her. A handful of newspapers had contacted her for an interview, and one day Jess was completely shocked to be called by someone working for the BBC asking if they could film her for an interview. Jess politely declined, she wanted her old quiet life back.

Overall though, Jess knew how lucky she was and made every effort to never complain. In fact she spent every day focusing on the positives and trying to never take anything for granted. She was especially enjoying this morning, which had started so perfectly.

Jess was rinsing off the conditioner in her hair when, out of nowhere, she could smell burning. Alarmed, thinking Matt may have burnt the breakfast, she shouted down to him. He must not have been able to hear her over the noise of the shower, because he did not respond.

She climbed out of the shower, wrapped a towel around herself and went downstairs. With every step she took she noticed that the smell was getting stronger.

"Matt? Are you ok?" she called out. By the time she reached the bottom of the stairs the smoke alarm started, which made her jump. She walked into the kitchen, to see the stove on, with a pan with smoke bellowing from it. She quickly moved the pan of food off the stove.

"Matt, you're going to burn the house down." She turned around to scold her partner, but instead all she could do was scream.

Standing in front of her was a badly scarred, grotesque Billy Bob, and next to him was Matt, lifeless, sitting in his chair with a wide slit across his neck and blood pouring all down his body.

Jess stood frozen, refusing to believe this was her reality. Billy Bob was covered in fresh burn scars that shone and covered most of his face. He had no hair at all and his skin was still bright red, raw and looked sore to touch. She looked over at Matt, who was still sitting in the chair, his head slumped back slightly but still facing her. She could not take her eyes off all the blood trickling from his neck, completely covering his front. There was no doubt about it, he was dead. Tears fell down her face uncontrollably, hoping that he had not suffered, and at the same time, deluding herself saying that he could still be saved.

"I have a piece of advice for you, Mrs Befria…" His voice was no longer the deep, powerful voice it had always been. It was now more of a raspy croak, masking unimaginable pain. "If you're going to kill someone, make sure they are in fact dead."

She forced herself to look away from Matt and back at the hideous murderer lunging towards her. She had no time to react. With one fell swoop Jess felt a stinging rip go through her throat. As she felt herself choking, she raised her hands to her neck. Only when she saw the knife in his hand and the blood on her own did she make the connection of what had just happened.

Desperately, she turned to run. Through sheer panic she was unaware of how much of her own blood was on the floor. She slipped and she crashed to the ground. Unable to break her own fall, she heard her head crack on the tiles.

On the floor she lay there, edging slowly into unconsciousness as blood pooled around her.

Matt could not save her this time. No one was here to save her. No clown to protect her and she could not help but feel like he never was. He used her for his own freedom, not caring what harm came her way.

Defeated, broken and dying she let the pain take over. Grateful at least she would not be conscious for what Billy Bob had planned for her next.

THE END